Crystal Saga

3 - Masquerade
4 - Discoveries

D. E. Weingand

Crystal Saga
3 - Masquerade
4 - Discoveries
A Crystal Saga Series

ISBN: 978-0-578-34966-4

Published by D. E. Weingand, Florence, Oregon 97439.

Printed in the United States of America.

Front cover photo by D. E. Weingand.

Luanna K. Leisure, Little White Feather
Graphic Artist and Independent Publisher.

To order additional books go to: **http://www.LuLu.com, Amazon.com or Barnesandnoble.com**

Email: weingand@me.com

Masquerade
A Crystal Saga Series
Book 3

Table of Contents

Discoveries
A Crystal Saga Series
Book 4

Table of Contents

Cast of Characters

Tamara...Heroine of Book 1 and beyond

Terra...Tamara's mother

Trident...Tamara's father and first a prince and then King of Marinea

Trina...Tamara's sister

Mia...Tamara's personal attendant

* * * * *

Super Children

Solange...Tamara's grandmother and a Super Daughter/Sister, advisor to the throne of Marinea. Has fair skin, and silver hair and eyes like Marineans. Wields white magic. Twin to Savea.

Savea... Super Daughter/Sister and Solange's twin, lives near a volcano. Has dark skin, hair and eyes unlike Marineans.

Sostor...a Super Son/Brother and ice magic mage on Mosshire. Ruler of the kingdom and twin to Sunan. Has fair skin, blonde hair and very blue eyes like residents of Mosshire.

Sunan…a Super Son/Brother and solar magic mage on Mesarra. Ruler of the kingdom and twin to Sostor. A solar magic mage. Has dark skin, hair and eyes like residents of Mesarra.

* * * * *

Dr. Astarte…a medical doctor serving the royal court

Dr. Angelus…a medical doctor and Doctor of Magical Studies in Marinea.

Commander Lockette. . .Leader of the newly-appointed Security Force.

Dana, Jon, and Borel. . .Members of the Security Force's Special Task Force.

Setting and Geography

Akura…the planet

Alteria…the land kingdom which succumbed to the Great Quakes and now is an island governed by a Council of Elders. Alterians have hazel eyes and blonde hair. No contact has been made with Marinea for generations.

Marinea…a kingdom under the sea formed after the Great Quakes divided the land kingdom of Alteria. Marineans have fair skin, silver hair and eyes and are governed by a king. They have retractable gills in order to live on both land and sea.

Mosshire…a land kingdom in the cold north composed of small pieces of forested and ice-covered land joined by bridges; ruled by Sostor, an ice magic mage. Residents have fair skin, blonde hair and very blue eyes.

Mesarra…a land kingdom in the south composed of a great desert. Residents are from tribes ruled by Sunan, a solar mage. Residents have very dark hair, skin and eyes.

Crystal Saga

3 - Masquerade

D. E. Weingand

Prologue

I am Tamara, the present Queen and ruler of the undersea kingdom of Marinea on the planet of Akura. I became ruler suddenly because my father, mother and younger sister, Trina, were kidnapped from the Bubble Train they were taking to the mainland kingdom of Alteria. My kingdom needed an interim ruler and I was next in the line of succession.

I was born with a crystal on my stomach. When I reached the age of puberty, my body added crystals to the palms of my hands and my forehead. No one could understand why the crystals appeared or why some of them suddenly began to change colors reflecting my emotions.

Our cosmology tells us that in the beginning of Time, the Creator sought to have company and made two Super Beings, one male and one female. These Super Beings in turn created a single male and a single female offspring of themselves. Having done that, they worried that those offspring might have too much power, so they decided to split each of the children into twin males and twin females. The two females, Solange and Savea, reside in my undersea kingdom. Savea lives close to several volcanos. Solange resides in the palace and has a special role: She is my grandmother!

The two males have two separate kingdoms: Sostor in the cold north and Sunan in the warm south. Each Super Being wears a crystal in a pendant. When all of this division took place, some crystal shards remained and a tornado whisked them away. No one knows why or where they were taken.

We held a reception when I became Queen and invited both Sunan and Sostor, as well as friends and dignitaries. It was interesting to watch the Brothers interact. They seemed to be polar opposites, like the lands they inhabit and rule. So far, I have not been able to determine if either of them has hostile intentions toward my kingdom or the Sisters, who are my partners in trying to understand my crystals and identify my related powers.

We have also been busy designing strategies to defend my kingdom and reclaim my family. We developed a three-prong strategy of offense and defense and are in the process of implementing it.

In Book 2, we had many adventures and struggles that we are all trying to understand. I was able to heal the Super Sisters of an imbalance. We do not know whether the Brothers have a similar imbalance.

I recently invited the Brothers to a ball celebrating my birthday. I wanted to have an opportunity to study them up close. My crystal powers aided me in this endeavor, and I thought that I understood them—but then a touch on their hands showed me that I was mistaken, and things are much more complex than I had realized. The only thing that I am fairly sure of is that one of the Super Brothers is my grandfather—but which one?

My family remains in captivity. I have had a vision that located them in Sostor's kingdom of Mosshire. Rescuing them is a top priority for me. The reason why they were kidnapped eludes me.

It seems that my life is full of challenges, both political and personal. All of the challenges seem to be connected to the cosmology that the Creator put into motion. I'm so glad that the Sisters are my allies. If they were not, I would feel so alone.

Chapter 1
The Sharing

Holding hands, Tamara and the Sisters walked across the Private Dining Room. Once they had made themselves comfortable on the couch, they looked at each other and smiled.

Solange spoke first, "Tamara, you have our attention—and our curiosity. Are you willing to share what you learned from your interaction with Dr. Angelus?"

"Of course," Tamara answered. "When he put me under a spell and I drifted across the room, even though my eyes were closed, my mind opened up and I could observe what had occurred with the Brothers. I knew I was watching a replay of a memory, but it looked like a program on a vid screen."

"So what did you see—and feel?" Savea asked."What we saw were rainbows streaming from the crystals on your palms."

"Actually, it was quite strange," acknowledged Tamara. "Although I could watch the scene unfold, the figures and their voices were dimmed, and what I heard was a truthful version of what they were thinking. It was as if what they said and thought was filtered to emit only the unvarnished truth."

"And what exactly was the truth that you heard?" inquired Solange.

"Sostor was focused on creating a magical persona that could hide his personal thoughts. He presented a very proper image of himself, but beneath it I could detect a devious and manipulative mind. He doesn't hate his Brother, but he wants to be better than him. There was a strong competitive undercurrent to his thinking. I think he would go to any lengths to make that happen,"Tamara added. "I think he would have been highly motivated to impregnate you, Solange."

"What about the 'two souls' that you detected earlier?" asked Savea. "You said there was an undercurrent of alarm and panic. Was there nothing good inside him?"

"I don't know," answered Tamara. "The magic was so strong that I couldn't penetrate it."

"Are you certain that the magic was generated by Sostor?" probed Savea.

"Are you suggesting that Sunan could somehow be creating Sostor's persona?" asked Tamara. "Is that even possible?"

"Frankly, I don't know what's possible," Savea admitted, "But I wouldn't rule anything out at this point. Now, what did you learn about Sunan?"

"Remember how I told you that I felt disjointed

fragments in him when I led him to the table?" asked Tamara. "They were so unlike the positive and hopeful sensations I experienced during the tornado that I caused as it lifted us into the air."

"Wait a minute," commanded Solange. "How do you know that YOU caused that tornado? What if Sunan was actually controlling the magic? You mentioned that under his warm and loving exterior were waves of cold ruthlessness. Consider, just for a minute, that Sostor could have been put under a spell and manipulated by Sunan. That could explain the alarm and panic you identified in Sostor. It would have been a masterful use of very powerful magic, if true."

"Which brings us back to the issue of an imbalance," Tamara reminded the Sisters. "When I eliminated your imbalance, you both were agreeable. In the case of the Brothers, their competitive spirit may have affected their imbalance differently. I think we have to acknowledge that both Brothers may have elements of imbalance, and that their core values might have been skewed to reflect personality traits that are not part of their essential natures. That could explain the duality I was sensing."

"I think you are on the right track," affirmed Savea. "If we have analyzed this correctly, what steps can we take to remedy the situation?"

“I think we’re forgetting something,” added Solange. “Sunan received a message and suddenly bolted from the room, citing an emergency back home. Let’s keep that in mind. It may be an important piece of this very challenging puzzle.”

“Good point,” agreed Tamara. “I don’t think we can proceed with this dilemma about the Brothers right now. Let’s move on to finishing our defense preparations and rescuing my family.”

Chapter 2
Finalizing Plans

Tamara asked the Sisters to accompany her to the garden next to the Ballroom. As they walked down a path edged with beautiful blooms, Savea picked a flower and inhaled its fragrance. Tucking it behind her ear, she inquired, "Tamara, this was a lovely idea, but is there another reason for leaving the Private Dining Room to continue our planning?"

"Yes," Tamara responded. "I was concerned about privacy. I've ordered our newly established Security Force to scan all the Palace rooms for listening devices. I've been uneasy ever since the Brothers departed. So much magic occurred during their visit that I suspect our conversations are being monitored."

"I think that was a wise move," agreed Solange. "As for me, I now question things I long held to be true as information keeps surfacing to turn my perception of reality on its head. For example, I can no longer be sure which of the Brothers visited me on my wedding night."

"I understand," Tamara agreed. "I expect a full report from the Security Chief tomorrow. In the meantime, I think we should behave as if someone is listening to everything we say inside the Palace."

"I agree," Savea joined in. "Shall we sit on that bench and begin to plan?"

"No," said Tamara. "That bench could have some kind of device that we are not aware of. I think we should keep walking in the open. I hope I'm not being paranoid."

"You're not. Being cautious and careful is not paranoia," assured Solange. "Savea, have you completed any part of your proposed actions?"

"Yes," Savea responded. "I've had the channel surrounding the kingdom dug, and lava is presently filling it. In addition, I have vaporized sufficient lava to complete a defensive dome over the kingdom as well. I believe we will be secure as soon as sufficient lava has filled the channel—which should be a matter of hours. Also, I am working on different offensive and defensive uses of weaponized lava to repel any incoming attacks."

"That's very good news!" exclaimed Tamara. "Solange, how far have you gotten?"

"As you know, since Savea and I were originally one being, I have some control over lava as well. Therefore, I have created a tunnel below the sea floor and constructed a track for the Bubble Train's route to the mainland of Alteria. The train should now have a secure and safe transit corridor," answered Solange. "And the airlock vulnerability between the ocean and the Palace Station was eliminated by Savea when she made the lava dome protecting the kingdom. The Security Force has been charged with creating a powerful password."

"More wonderful news!" Tamara enthused. "I'm so pleased."

"And I had planned to partner with Sunan to save my son," added Solange, "but after our interactions with the Brothers, I no longer think that would be a good idea. We need to design a different approach."

"Definitely," stressed Savea. "Do either of you have any ideas?"

Tamara extended her arms and said, "I've been working hard at understanding what my powers can do. I don't believe the Brothers are really aware of the true extent of these powers—even I have been surprised over and over again. We must be very careful to only discuss them in the open air. They are likely to be our secret weapon.

"I am increasingly impressed with how my crystals are able to empower my bracelets, both defensively and offensively. It might be a good idea for me to practice with both of you so we can determine if and how much my crystals and bracelets can deflect the power of your crystal pendants."

"That's an excellent idea," affirmed Solange. "Let's agree to start that first thing in the morning."

As the three women returned inside the palace, they didn't notice that certain plants turned to follow their progress.

Chapter 3
Enter The Security Force

When Tamara awoke the next day, there was a discreet knock at her bedroom door. "Enter," Tamara responded.

Mia came in and bowed. "Your Majesty," she said, "Commander Lockette of the Security Force has asked for an audience."

"Thank you, Mia," Tamara replied. "Please tell him I will meet him in his office in thirty minutes."

Mia bowed, turned, and left the room to deliver the message.

* * * * *

Tamara finished dressing, brushed her hair and made her way to the Security Force office. Commander Lockette met her at the door, bowed, and asked her to take a seat.

"Good morning, Your Majesty," said Commander Lockette. "I appreciate your promptness."

"This meeting is long overdue," responded Tamara. "I apologize for not coming sooner, but the kingdom has been in a bit of a turmoil. Am I correct to assume that you were hired by my grandmother, Solange?"

"Yes," replied the Commander. "When your father

assumed the throne after the presumed death of your grandfather, your grandmother had been managing the kingdom along with Savea for some time. Since the royal death was never verified, your grandmother hired me as a bodyguard for your father."

"Bodyguard! Was his life in danger?" asked Tamara.

"We didn't know," answered the Commander, "But your grandmother was concerned for his safety."

"Please excuse the bluntness of my next question," said Tamara. "Since I was unaware of your presence on the staff, can you bring me up to date on your qualifications for both the bodyguard position and your advancement to Head of the new Security Force?"

"Of course, Your Majesty," he replied. "Your question is entirely relevant and not unexpected. I had a successful martial arts training business and applied for the palace position when it became available. I sold my business when I was selected to be one of your father's bodyguards. I also hold an advanced degree in magical arts, which I believe might have been the deciding factor in my selection."

"You have an interesting background," commented Tamara. "Can I assume that you were thoroughly vetted as a part of your application?"

"Definitely," he affirmed. "It was a very extensive

process. And I was vetted again when I applied for my present position."

"Since you were one of my father's bodyguards, why didn't you accompany him on his trip to the mainland?" asked Tamara.

"That was your father's decision. Since Alteria is populated by non-magicals, he preferred to take only non-magical staff with him. I was devastated when the kidnapping happened. When the Security Force was formed, I applied to lead it so that I could focus resources on rescuing him."

"Do you know if all members of the palace staff have been thoroughly vetted?" she inquired.

"I do not. But I'll look into that. It should be standard practice before any hire," he added.

"I definitely agree," Tamara affirmed. "I would be particularly interested in the two doctors that serve in the Palace: Dr. Astarte and Dr. Angelus. They have been involved in some highly classified discussions.

"By the way, when you were studying magical arts, did you cross paths with Dr. Angelus? He claims to have an advanced degree in that field."

"Not that I remember. I'll put him at the top of my list. With your permission, I would like to turn now to the reason that I requested this audience. My team has been testing the various defenses that the Sisters have put into place. I am pleased to inform you that they seem very effective," asserted the Commander.

"I am delighted to hear it," Tamara replied with a smile. During their conversation, she couldn't help noticing the Commander's professional demeanor, accented by his neatly arranged silver hair and piercing blue eyes. He appeared to be approximately her age, but that was often difficult to ascertain in Marinean natives.

"I have another request of you," added Tamara. "I am concerned that listening devices may have been placed around the Palace. I need you to do a thorough initial sweep and then repeat sweeps at regular intervals."

"Do you wish me to conduct sweeps both inside and outside the Palace?" he asked.

"I do," she affirmed. "The Super Brothers have just exited the kingdom, and I want to know if we are secure."

"I will begin immediately," promised the Commander. "I will use both standard and magical investigative measures. I should have a report within a few days."

"Thank you," Tamara said as the Commander escorted her to the door.

* * * * *

Later that day, Tamara met the Sisters in the garden.

"Let's stroll down to the boat dock and enjoy the afternoon by taking a short boat ride."

The Sisters agree and the trio boarded a spacious, driverless pontoon craft that was designed to follow an underwater track. As the boat began to move, Tamara took an audio device from her pocket, turning on music to a high volume.

"What are you doing?" asked Savea.

"Until the Security Force completes the scan for listening devices, I want us to only discuss strategies on this boat with loud music covering our voices. I've also had bubble headgear placed aboard. We will be able to communicate with each other," explained Tamara.

"That seems wise," agreed Solange. "We can't be too careful," she observed as she placed a bubble on her head.

"The Security Force Commander has assured me that our lava-based defense strategies are working and are secure. That was a great relief," commented Tamara. "Now it's time to develop a plan to rescue my family."

"I would like to re-introduce my idea to create another tunnel that would extend between Marinea and Mosshire," said Savea. "I could lead a small tactical group from the Security Force through the tunnel and stage a surprise rescue attempt."

"We would have to gather more intel to determine the

precise location of my family and the best time to launch the attempt," advised Tamara. "I will try to induce another vision in myself to add to our knowledge. Also, the Commander would have to approve the plan," she added.

"I'm afraid we are being premature out of love for my son and his family," worried Solange. "I don't feel that they are in imminent danger. I'm more concerned about the Brothers and deciphering how their powers are distributed between them. I really feel that figuring that out is crucial to our success."

"Savea, I believe your plan is a good one, and I agree with Solange that we need more intel first—including a better understanding of the Brothers," opined Tamara. "Since Solange feels that we have some time to gather resources, I think waiting for reports from the Security Force would be beneficial.

"I expect some reports within days," she added. "I'll let you know as soon as I receive them."

Chapter 4
The Security Force Reports

Several days later, Tamara received an urgent message from the Commander requesting her presence in his office as soon as possible.

As she entered, he rose and directed her to a nearby chair. "Your Majesty," he began, "I have several reports for you. You will find some disturbing. But first, I wish to commend you for your decision to confine sensitive conversations to the boat, using music as a cover and bubble headgear to communicate. That was very wise."

"Thank you. We are trying to be circumspect," she said.

"Given what our investigations have discovered, I am pleased that you instituted those precautions," commented the Commander. "I can give you the results of some investigations now, but others are still in process."

"What can you tell me at this point?" Tamara asked.

"The vetting of all palace staff members is underway and will take some time because of the number of staff," the Commander began. "However, I did begin with the two doctors, as you requested. Dr. Astarte has been the court physician the longest, and her background is excellent. I found nothing suspicious."

"However, Dr. Angelus is a recent hire, presumably to aid Dr. Astarte with her busy schedule. But I can find no trace of him prior to starting his position at the Palace. My contacts in magical arts could not produce any evidence that he had ever studied the subject, and there is no sign that he received a degree in it. I must conclude that he is not who he says he is. I haven't yet discovered how Dr. Angelus came to be selected to work in the Palace," he added. "I believe you and I should interview Dr. Astarte to ascertain what, if any, sensitive information she has shared with him—and if she knows why and by whom he was hired."

"I totally agree," affirmed Tamara. "Let's do just that after our conversation here is completed."

"Moving on to the issue of potential listening devices," continued the Commander, "it pains me to tell you that they are everywhere, both inside and outside of the Palace. Someone is very interested in you and the Sisters and what you may be planning. How much have you discussed that has undoubtedly been overheard?"

"Oh my goodness!" Tamara exclaimed. "So much. It is only our latest conversation that was handled with caution. And when Sunan was here, he took part in our discussions. What do we do now?"

"In situations like this, the first step is to sow disinformation that will cancel out what those who have been listening think they know," responded the Commander. "I would recommend that you and the Sisters meet with me and I will bring up reasons why what you are planning cannot work. Plus, please continue to hold your real conversations on the boat."

"Most of our planning has been in the Private Dining Room," admitted Tamara. "Were listening devices found there?"

"Unfortunately, there are many—both magical and non-magical. Therefore, I think we should hold our false meeting there," he suggested. "While my staff will be removing or neutralizing all devices that we have located, I will instruct them to let the ones in the Private Dining Room remain.

"Now, I have a question for you. Other than conversations on the boat, where else outside the palace have you discussed plans with the Sisters?" asked the Commander.

"I thought I was being careful by taking walks in the garden. I had the impression that in the open air, we were safe," confessed Tamara.

"Sadly, you were not," informed the Commander. "Have you ever heard of faux plants?" he asked.

"No, what are they?" Tamara answered.

"They are false plants, very realistic, but robotic in nature. I cast a discovery spell over the entire garden and it was amazing how many plants, flowers and shrubs began to glow. The garden is infested with listening devices," he continued. "Once we eliminate them, the entire garden will need to be replanted," he added.

Tamara put her hands to her temples and sighed, "My head is starting to hurt. How and why has this happened? And who has done it?"

"Those are complicated questions, Your Majesty," the Commander stated, "But have no fear—we will find the answers for you. Shall we now go and pay Dr. Astarte a visit?" he asked. Rising, Tamara took the Commander's arm, and they began to walk to Dr. Astarte's office.

* * * * *

Commander Lockette knocked softly at Dr. Astarte's door. In a moment, the doctor admitted them into her office and gestured to chairs facing her desk.

"Welcome, Your Majesty and … I'm afraid we haven't met."

"Dr. Astarte, this is Commander Lockette, the Head of our new Security Force," said Tamara. "We have some questions that we hope you can help us with."

"I'll do my best, Your Majesty," promised Dr. Astarte.

"How much do you know about Dr. Angelus?" asked the Commander. "Can you share what you know about why he was hired, who recommended him and what qualifications he has?"

"My goodness, has he done something wrong?" Dr. Astarte asked.

"Whatever you tell us will remain confidential, I assure you," stressed the Commander. "We do need answers to our questions."

"Well, as you may know, I have been Court Physician for some time. I came on board during the reign of the King—your father, Your Majesty," she began.

"To clarify, Dr. Astarte," prodded the Commander, "You were appointed by King Trident?"

"Yes," she replied. "But I was hired by letter."

"Didn't that strike you as a bit odd?" the Commander pressed.

"Actually, it did at the time," she responded, "but I had just completed my medical training and I was grateful for the opportunity."

"At the time of Dr. Angelus' appointment, was your workload too high? Is that the reason for his hire?" asked Tamara.

"Not at all," answered the doctor. "In fact, I was

surprised. I came to work one day and he was just there."

"Do you know who hired him?" asked the Commander. "And what do you know about his background?"

"He showed me a letter offering him the position. It was signed by your father, Your Majesty," she answered. "I assumed that it was legitimate. He told me he had degrees in both medicine and the magical arts. However, I really don't know anything about him."

"Do you work well together? Have you shared anything about me or the Sisters with him?" asked Tamara.

"I don't work with him at all. He's a very private person. But no, I am a strict believer in doctor-patient privilege, and I've not shared anything about the three of you with him," she stressed.

"Has he ever asked questions about us?" Tamara pursued.

"Indeed he has. He seems very curious about the three of you. But I promise that I've never given him any information."

"This may seem like an odd question," Tamara continued, "But does he seem a real, actual person? Or do you sense anything odd?"

"I'm not sure," the doctor answered. "When he visited you last, he returned shaking his head and started paging through some spell books that he had brought with him. Oh, there was one time when I was updating patient files and looked up when he entered my office. For just a moment, I thought my eyes were playing tricks on me because he seemed a bit out of focus. I blamed it on overwork and fatigue, but since you are asking, is something wrong here?"

"That's what we're trying to figure out," responded the Commander. "May we have your assurance that nothing spoken in this meeting will be shared with anyone?"

"Of course," she replied. "And I'll keep an eye on him." She walked her guests to the door and said, "Welcome to the Palace, Commander."

Commander Lockette removed a device from his pocket and flashed a light at the doctor. Then he and Tamara left together.

"What did you just do?" asked Tamara.

"I used a special device to erase her memory of our conversation. Just as a precaution," he replied.

"I was wondering if you had removed the listening devices from her office," she queried.

"Oh yes," he said, "That was one of my first actions once I determined that we would be visiting her. What did you think of our meeting?"

"More informative than I expected," she replied. "I

need to brief you on recent developments that occurred before you arrived. Would you like to go on a boat ride?"

Chapter 5
The Boat Ride

Tamara and the Commander strolled down to the boat dock, arm in arm. When they arrived, they were greeted by Solange and Savea, who were already on board.

As she stepped onto the boat, Tamara turned on the music device that she was holding, passed out bubble headgear and greeted the Sisters, "I would like you to meet the new Head of our Security Force, Commander Lockette. He has already made great strides in improving our overall security."

The Commander bowed to the Sisters and commended them for their many years of service to the kingdom. "Commander," Solange interrupted, "You look familiar. Have we met?"

"Not formally," answered the Commander. "But I was one of your son's bodyguards until quite recently."

"But you didn't go with him on the Bubble Train?" asked Solange.

"No," the Commander responded. "As I told the Queen, King Trident preferred to take a staff of non-magicals with him to the non-magical mainland. I was horrified by what happened, and it compelled me to apply to head the Security

Force."

After everyone had made themselves comfortable and put on the bubble headgear, the boat automatically began to move on its track. Tamara turned up the volume on the music device in preparation for their discussion.

Tamara asked the Sisters to be completely candid while briefing the Commander so that he would be made aware of all that had taken place in their various investigations thus far. The Commander listened intently, occasionally asking for clarification. When the Sisters finished, Tamara proceeded to demonstrate some of her powers, which astonished the Commander.

"I had heard rumors about your crystals," he said. "But I had no idea what they could do! You have an impressive defensive and offensive arsenal."

"And I try to keep a low profile so that our enemies cannot know. That's why I was so worried about listening devices," she stated. "Now it's your turn to share with the Sisters what your team has found so far."

As the boat continued on its automatic track, the Commander outlined in detail what his staff had discovered concerning the listening devices. "All the devices except those in the Private Dining Room have either been removed or disabled," he asserted. "We have deliberately left those in place because they will play a critical role in our disinformation campaign."

"What exactly is a disinformation campaign?" asked Savea.

"It's a strategy to sow false information to undermine intelligence operations and counter any real facts that may be known," the Commander answered. "As soon as possible, I want to meet with all of you in the Private Dining Room where you will brief me in general terms on what you are planning and I will present arguments as to why they will not work. Hopefully, the listening devices are being monitored by the enemy and my arguments against the efficacy of your plans will prove both confusing and persuasive."

"That's genius!" exclaimed Solange. "Why don't we meet in the Private Dining Room for breakfast tomorrow morning? Will that work for you, Commander?"

"It will," he replied. "I'll create a list of arguments tonight and be ready to be an obstructionist in the morning. Just remember to be careful in your conversation at breakfast. It must sound normal and yet offer no information."

As the boat turned and headed back to the dock, Tamara asked the Commander, "Please summarize our conversation with Dr. Astarte for the Sisters. Since they have also interacted with Dr. Angelus, I'd like to hear what they think."

The Commander briefly related the facts from the meeting with Dr. Astarte. He stopped short of reaching any conclusions until the Sisters had an opportunity to weigh the evidence independently.

At the end of his report, Solange sighed and said, "I'm saddened by what you have related. Clearly, there is a similarity between Dr. Angelus and my former husband. I don't know what magic or technology was employed, but both men appear to be artificial in some way."

"How do we handle Dr. Angelus moving forward," asked Savea. "There will be suspicions if we ignore him completely."

"As a first step, I plan to bring him to my office to introduce myself and 'get to know him.' I'm pretty good at subtle interrogation," the Commander added.

"How soon do you intend to do that?" inquired Tamara.

"Right after breakfast tomorrow. I don't think it would be wise to delay any of our counter measures," he added emphatically.

As the boat reached the dock, everyone disembarked and Tamara retrieved her music device. Waving goodbye to everyone, she walked back to the Palace and retired for the evening.

Chapter 6
The Disinformation Breakfast

As morning approached, Tamara's sleep began to be disturbed. She tossed and turned, becoming increasingly agitated. Her palm crystals began to shoot rainbows around the room; the crystals on her forehead and stomach turned bright red. Even her hair changed from white to red.

"Mia!" she cried out as she sat up in bed trembling.

In a few minutes, Mia entered the room and ran to her. "What has happened, Your Majesty?" she asked as she held Tamara in her arms. "You are as cold as ice."

"I had such a terrible dream," sobbed Tamara. "My family had been transferred to what looked like prison cells, and they were shivering. I'm so afraid that their lives are in danger."

Mia hurried to the intercom on the wall and placed a call to Solange. "Come quickly," she urged.

Within a few minutes, Solange burst through the door and ran to Tamara's side. Wiping the tears from Tamara's face, she instructed her to breathe deeply so her emotions could calm. Gradually, Tamara's crystals and hair faded to normal and the rainbows dissipated. "Now describe to me exactly what you saw in your dream," Solange said.

"It was different than a dream. It was more like a vision," said Tamara. "I saw my family in a cold jail cell. They were shivering and holding each other. There were guards outside the cell, poking at them with spears and laughing! Then Sostor came into view. He was yelling at Father, who was ignoring him. Mother had her arms around Trina, and Father appeared to be comforting them. Trina looked so scared. None of them was wearing furs like before. They were wearing what they had on when they boarded the train. Sostor began waving a piece of paper at Father and tried to hand him a pen, which Father refused to take. One of the guards entered the cell and grabbed Trina's arm. Father extended his hands and blue light hit the guard—who disappeared. Then I woke up screaming."

"Tamara, did you notice how Sostor and your father were reacting during this vision?" asked Solange.

Tamara closed her eyes and tried to replay the vision in her memory. "Sostor was angry that Father wouldn't sign whatever was on that paper until Father raised his hands and the blue light made the guard vanish—then Father looked shocked and frightened. Father had been comforting Mother and Trina and became angry when the guard grabbed Trina's arm—then when the blue light shot out from his hands, he appeared to be astonished."

"I'm not surprised," commented Solange. "Remember that none of us had any idea that your father was capable of magic up to this point, but Sunan did remind us that while you are a descendent of the female Super Being line, your father is a descendent of the male line."

"That's right," Tamara agreed. "I had forgotten about that. I think we should return to the boat after our breakfast meeting to consider this further in private. I'll join you for breakfast in a few minutes."

After Solange and Mia left the room, Tamara dressed for the day and looked at her reflection in the mirror. To her surprise, another crystal had appeared on her forehead. "Another mystery to be solved," she thought as she combed her hair over her forehead and left to meet the others at breakfast.

* * * * *

Entering the Private Dining Room, Tamara chose a seat between Solange and Savea. "Thank you for agreeing to a short breakfast meeting. I'd like to review what we have planned so far and get an opinion from the Commander as to feasibility. Savea, would you please begin?"

"Certainly," replied Savea. "The first part of my plan was to excavate a large ditch around the kingdom and direct lava into it."

"That sounds good on paper," said the Commander. "But consider what would happen if a significant earthquake should occur. Lava would spill out in many directions and perhaps destroy part of the kingdom. I strongly recommend that you rethink this strategy."

"My second idea was to vaporize lava and fashion it into a protective dome over the kingdom to deflect any incoming assault," added Savea.

"I must repeat my caution against this idea as well. We are under the sea and such a dome would be subject to the effects of ocean tides and earth movements. I'd recommend a closer look at possible consequences," stressed the Commander.

"Oh dear," complained Savea, "That would mean starting all over."

"I'm afraid so," murmured Solange. "My thoughts weren't nearly as advanced technologically as yours, Savea. We need to rethink everything, and quickly. Right now, we are in a very vulnerable position."

"I agree with the need for urgency and will help in any way I can," offered the Commander. "Right now, I think we should order breakfast and, when properly refreshed, take a walk through the garden to clear our minds."

"That sounds like an excellent proposition,

Commander," agreed Tamara, calling a server over to take their orders.

* * * * *

Sometime later, after enjoying a leisurely breakfast with no further substantive discussion, Tamara and her guests walked swiftly through the garden down to the boat dock. Tamara turned on the music as everyone donned their bubble headgear. They sat close to each other in order to keep their voices low.

"Do you think we were effective?" she asked the Commander.

"I'm fairly positive that the bait has been put out there," he replied. "If it worked, then I believe we can expect an attack in the near future. I'm going to schedule a false 'training exercise' for tomorrow in order to ready my troops. I've been actively recruiting magicals to the Force in anticipation of such an attack. And as soon as I get back to my office, I will invite Dr. Angelus in for a chat."

"That sounds wonderful," approved Tamara. "You seem to have things well in hand."

Savea interjected, "I want to add that I found your 'disinformation' curiously persuasive. I need to reexamine my defenses and add magical elements with my powers to counter any earthquake or other magical effects coming from the enemy."

"I concur," said Solange. "I plan to strengthen my contribution with magical enhancement as well. Thank you, Commander, for 'disinformation' that actually seems to be useful to us."

"How interesting that your 'disinformation' has practical benefits for us," commented Tamara. "Now, I want to brief you on my dream or vision of early this morning."

Savea leaned forward to listen to Tamara's account of the vision. Solange leaned back to observe everyone since she had already heard Tamara's description earlier. She noted with interest the looks of alarm on the faces of Savea and the Commander.

* * * * *

Commander Lockette stood and began to pace the deck. "Your vision is quite disturbing," he said. "I'm worried that an attack may occur earlier than I had anticipated. And King Trident's sudden display of magic is a wild card. Do you think he has any control of this power? Is there any way to communicate with him?"

Tamara answered, "I don't know. And as someone who is constantly trying to understand personal powers, both known and unknown," she said, pulling her hair aside and showing the second crystal on her forehead, "It can be both frustrating and challenging."

The Commander and the Sisters gasped at Tamara's revelation. Solange asked, "When did you notice that second crystal?"

Tamara admitted, "Just before I came to breakfast, when I was combing my hair. And I have no idea what it can do."

Chapter 7
Next Steps

Commander Lockette sat at his desk pondering various options that confronted him. He rang for his aide, who knocked at his door a few minutes later.

"Have a seat, Sergeant," said the Commander. "We need to discuss some logistics. I have some new information that requires that we begin our training exercises tomorrow. Please notify the Security Force members that we will commence immediately after breakfast tomorrow."

"Yes, Sir," responded the aide. "Is there anything else I need to know about this change of plan?"

"No," answered the Commander. "Let's just say that intel suggests that we need to be ready for a hostile incursion sooner rather than later. Oh, and please ask Dr. Angelus to come in on your way out."

"Aye, sir," replied the aide as he saluted and left the office.

* * * * *

A sharp knock at the door alerted the Commander to his next visitor. "Enter," he directed.

Dr. Angelus walked into the office. "You wished to see

me?" he inquired.

"Indeed," responded the Commander. "I like to welcome all new hires and I apologize for my delay in greeting you. Please have a seat and make yourself comfortable.

"I'm relatively new in this position myself and I've had a lot to deal with. Please tell me about your background and your plans for the future."

"I am hoping to take advantage of my somewhat unique background," said Dr. Angelus. "Since I have degrees in both medicine and magical arts, I believe I can be useful in a variety of situations."

"Where did you matriculate, and when did you graduate?" asked the Commander.

"I've held several positions since then and the exact dates slip my mind," replied the doctor. *"Nice diversion,"* thought the Commander.

"I can understand that," sympathized the Commander. "But what educational institutions did you attend? I'm wondering if we could have crossed paths."

"I don't think so," replied the doctor. "I'm sure I would have remembered you." *"More diversion,"* thought the Commander. *"I wonder how I can get a real answer."*

"How did you find out about an opening here in the palace?" asked the Commander.

"A friend sent me a message and encouraged me to apply. The position I was in was only temporary," the doctor added.

"May I have the name of your friend?"

"I'm afraid that I promised to keep his identity confidential," asserted the doctor. "It falls under doctor-patient privilege." *"This doctor is skilled at misdirection,"* thought the Commander.

"I'm afraid that I must insist on having answers to my questions," demanded the Commander. "If you don't comply, I will have to detain you until you do."

The Commander looked sternly at the doctor and was startled when the doctor's image began to blur. As he continued to study the doctor, the image shivered, faded, and eventually disappeared. Calling for his aide, he moved quickly to where the doctor had been sitting and moved his hand through where the doctor had been. There was nothing.

The aide came in and asked with surprise where the doctor was. "Did you see him leave?" asked the Commander.

"No sir," the aide replied. "I was outside the door the entire time."

"That will be all, Sergeant," dismissed the Commander. When the aide had left, the Commander began to chant slowly, waving his hands in and through the space the doctor had occupied. A green haze appeared in that space, gradually taking the shape of the doctor. "*Ah, I have you*," thought the Commander.

Continuing to chant, but in a different tone, the Commander increased the volume and clapped his hands. The mist solidified and the doctor was once again sitting in the chair.

"That was a nice trick," the Commander commented. "Now, you are confined to that chair and ordered to respond truthfully to my questions. My first question is: Who and what are you?"

In a mechanical voice, the doctor responded while the image blurred but remained in the chair. "I am a magical reproduction of a now deceased physician."

"And you possess both medical and magical properties?" asked the Commander.

"I do."

"Who created you?"

"I am not allowed to divulge that information."

"I have ordered you to respond truthfully to all my questions," reminded the Commander.

"I will permanently self-destruct if I do so."

"We will come back to that question. What is your purpose in taking a position in the palace?"

"To gather information."

"Information about what or whom?"

"Information about defenses and the Queen."

"Have you gathered this information?'

"Yes."

"Have you transmitted it?"

"Yes."

"What was this information?"

"Defenses using lava and the Queen's extraordinary powers."

"Where did you send this information?"

"I'm not allowed to say."

"Your ability to disappear—why did you use it?"

"So I wouldn't have to answer your questions."

"How do you get your instructions?"

"They were given to me before I was activated."

"If I were to release you right now, what would you do?"

"I would self-destruct."

The Commander waved his hand and a bubble encased the doctor. Calling his aide, the Commander instructed, "Remove this immobilized avatar and place it in solitary confinement. Then send a message to the Queen and ask her to meet me at the boat."

Chapter 8
Updating Plans

As Tamara hastened to the boat, she wondered about the urgency of the Commander's summons. Climbing aboard, she located the Commander by the front railing.

"I'm here, Commander," she announced as she activated her music device and donned bubble headgear.

"Please sit down, Your Majesty," he invited. "We need to accelerate our timetable."

"What has happened?" she asked.

"Can you remember what took place when you used your powers in the presence of Dr. Angelus?" asked the Commander as he paced back and forth.

"What I remember most clearly is the time I sent for him after Sunan left to return to his kingdom. I had touched the hands of both brothers at lunch and I asked the doctor to help me retrieve that memory. He began chanting as I reclined on a couch in the Private Dining Room. He said it would release the memory of that incident and that I would retain the memory after he was finished. However, the Sisters later told me that a golden haze appeared from his hands and surrounded me. I began to levitate and rainbows emerged from the crystals on my palms. Then my body began rotating slowly and my bracelets began to glow, absorbing the golden haze, and I drifted back to the couch. What was unexpected is that the resultant memory had been purified by the bracelets and I could tell truth from falsehoods. Dr. Angelus looked astonished and requested permission to withdraw and ponder what he had seen."

"Hmm…more likely he wanted to report what he had seen," commented the Commander.

"What are you saying?" asked Tamara. "Have you had your interview with the doctor?"

The Commander took a seat next to Tamara and related what he had learned from that interview. As she listened, her face paled and she inquired, "Where is the doctor now?"

"After he attempted to escape, I encased him in a confining bubble and had my aide secure him in a solitary confinement cell. But since he admitted that information had been sent to whomever was his handler, I had to be certain that he was isolated and unable to have further contact. Also, his intent to self-destruct must be taken seriously."

"I'm shocked," sighed Tamara. "I had trusted him completely. I don't feel that I can rely on my judgment of people anymore."

"Please don't think ill of yourself, Your Majesty," said the Commander persuasively. "The doctor was a very sophisticated and well-designed magical operative. We are facing a type of enemy that is unfamiliar to us, and we have to prepare our strategies accordingly. We need to assume that nothing may be as it seems."

* * * * *

"Would you like a beverage, Your Majesty?" asked the Commander. "I have arranged for the Sisters to join us here shortly. As I mentioned when you arrived, I believe that we must step up our plans in light of this new information about the doctor."

"Thank you, Commander. A beverage would be most welcome," answered Tamara. "And I can see the Sisters coming toward the dock. Your timing is noteworthy."

Once the Sisters had boarded the boat, Tamara and the Commander shared with them what had been discovered about the doctor. Solange was upset and said she regretted her naiveté. Savea raged about treason and the lack of morality in the enemy they faced.

Solange turned to the Commander and asked, "What do we do now? And how can we identify the culprit behind this attack—and it is an attack on our kingdom."

"We must quickly implement our defenses. As we move

forward, more evidence concerning the perpetrator will come into view," added the Commander. "Sisters, how soon can your plans go into effect?"

Savea spoke first, "I can have everything operative in two days," she promised. "I am so angry that I will make that happen."

"I think two days is a reasonable goal," affirmed Solange. "As for my plans, the tunnel for the Bubble Train is completed and the train is scheduled to begin using it tomorrow. I have not yet begun to construct the tunnel leading to Mosshire. I wanted to ask you, Commander, when you believe I should do so. I worry that, while we would gain access to Mosshire, the tunnel would also allow an invasion to head in our direction."

"You are correct," affirmed the Commander. "Is there any way that such a tunnel could be hidden from prying eyes? Could additional defenses be installed within the tunnel?"

"I've been thinking along those lines," Solange agreed. "Commander, please keep us apprised of any further intel, and I would appreciate your advice about how to make such a tunnel a tactical advantage for us while deterring any incursion from Mosshire."

"I would be pleased to work with you, Solange," promised the Commander. "In fact, since time is quickly running out for planning, would you be willing to stay on the boat once this meeting has concluded?"

"Of course," Solange replied. "I have some ideas that I would like to present to you."

"Will your Security Force be at full strength in two days, Commander?" asked Tamara. "And will their training be complete?"

"Yes to both questions, Your Majesty," responded the Commander. "They have been training diligently and are very skilled. I should add that I have been hiring additional members who have magical capabilities. Given what we now know, I think those talents will be particularly important.

"One more thing," added the Commander. "Your Majesty, have you figured out what the second crystal on your forehead can do?"

"Sadly, no," Tamara responded. "However, my crystals seem to announce themselves when they are needed."

Chapter 9
The Second Tunnel

After Savea and Tamara left the meeting, the Commander poured beverages for Solange and himself. Turning to her, he asked, "You mentioned that you had some ideas. Let's begin our discussion with those."

"Tunneling to Mosshire would not be a straightforward project like the tunnel for the Bubble Train," she began. "The sounds of construction would have to be silenced, for example. I was also thinking that an invisibility spell would be a good idea in order to hide the tunnel's existence."

"Those are excellent points," approved the Commander. "Can your powers accomplish those goals?"

"Yes," affirmed Solange. "But depending on Sostor's magical skills, my efforts could be reversed."

"That's why disinformation is so important. If he is misled about our intentions and kept in the dark about what has already been accomplished, we should hopefully be okay. If he does discover what we are doing, that's why our defenses must be activated as soon as possible. Do you have any suggestions about defenses?"

"Not yet," she responded. "I was hoping that you

might have some thoughts along those lines."

"What comes to mind are booby traps," he offered, "such as arrows fired from walls, floors that drop away if the right tiles aren't stepped on correctly, or explosive devices. What do you think?"

"If we add magic, we can be more creative—and lethal," she commented.

"That's true," he agreed. "When I get back to my office I'll create a task force of some of the newly hired magicals. They seem like a clever bunch and have been thoroughly vetted. I'll get back to you with some of their ideas tomorrow."

* * * * *

The next morning, the Commander sent word to Solange to meet him at the boat.

When Solange arrived, she was surprised to find Savea and Tamara already there. "I didn't know you were coming," she remarked.

"After the Commander sent you a message, he decided that we should all be present," explained Tamara. "I agree with his judgment. I think I see him coming now. I've already activated my music device. Remember to put on your bubble headgear."

"Good morning, Commander," Tamara greeted him. "You have company, I see."

"These are some members of my Special Task Force," he explained. "I thought it best to have them present their ideas directly. May I present Dana, Jon, and Borel."

"Thank you all for coming. We appreciate your efforts in so swiftly devising possible enhancements to our defenses," affirmed Tamara.

Dana began the report, "We all agree that the misinformation generated by the Commander will likely stimulate an attack sooner rather than later. Since the enemy hopefully believes that we are unprepared and vulnerable, that attack is likely to be airborne. How confident are you that the lava dome can withstand such an attack?"

Savea responded, "Very confident. I have added a series of strengthening spells to the original design. In addition, I created retaliatory pods within the dome that will respond to any assault."

Dana nodded approvingly, "Both measures are wise. But we would like to recommend a second dome covering the first. Such a dome should contain your retaliatory pods and be cloaked with an invisibility spell. In other words, the original dome would be defensive and the dome we suggest adding would be offensive."

Savea clapped her hands and cried, "I love it! That's a perfect enhancement."

Jon spoke next. “That moat or ditch surrounding the kingdom has a major drawback. When lava is flowing, it is a definite deterrent. But lava eventually cools and becomes solid. At that point it could be crossed easily. We did some research and would like to recommend adding a little-known spell to the lava that would prevent it from solidifying.”

Savea looked surprised, “I am unaware of such a spell. Where did you find it?”

“Among the members of the Task Force, we have amassed quite a collection of obscure works. We found it incredibly useful in developing recommendations for you.”

“You are correct that lava does eventually cool. We are indebted to you for your scholarship and ingenuity,” praised Savea.

“We hope you find our final ideas as useful,” interrupted Borel. “We had vigorous discussions for several hours about the pros and cons of a tunnel to Mosshire. If discovered, that could be viewed as an aggressive act leading to war. Our challenge was to focus on defensive measures that could be altered into offensive measures if needed. The Commander shared his knowledge of old-fashioned booby traps, and we used it as a stimulus for our brainstorming.”

Dana added, “Those old booby traps encouraged us to think way outside the box and come up with unheard of mechanisms of defense."

"In fact, we stayed up arguing and plotting all night!" cried Jon. "This is what we propose," he said, producing a vid screen. "We have designed a tunnel in sections, with numerous trap doors scattered along its length and magical rays hidden in the walls. Between each section are gates that can descend and block any movement, but they are masked by an invisibility spell. If an intruder hits one, debilitating shock beams will activate. A member of the Security Force would know how to disable the gates and would be unaffected."

"And the tunnel itself," added Borel, "could be built on an underground river of liquefied lava, separated from the tunnel by a layer of cooling insulation to protect Security Force members within the tunnel. If a hostile agent jumped onto a gate or into a wall, a trap door would plunge that person down into the lava river."

"I'm so impressed with the enhancements that you and your team have suggested," applauded Tamara.

"Please extend our gratitude to everyone who has worked on this project. Solange and Savea, you previously estimated that these defenses could be completed in two days. Now we are at the one day mark. How much more time do you need to be prepared for an attack?" asked Tamara.

Savea looked at the Task Force members and inquired,

"Would you and your colleagues work with us to implement those ideas?" All three nodded assent. "Then I believe this nexus of magical talent should be able to complete our mission in one more extra day." Wreathed in smiles, the Sisters and Task Force members disembarked and hurried to the Palace to begin their work.

Tamara and the Commander gazed after them with worry on their faces. "What if an extra day is one day more than we have?" sighed Tamara.

"I'm heading back to my office to check for new intel," the Commander said. "Would you like to accompany me?"

"Absolutely," she agreed. "The clock is ticking."

Chapter 10
Turning Plans into Actions

Tamara sank into a chair in the Commander's office. She watched the Commander's face as he reviewed the latest reports. Fatigue began to claim her and she dropped into a drowsy state. Startled, she sat up straight and exclaimed, "No! It's too soon!"

The Commander hurried to her side and asked, "What is wrong? What did you see?"

"I saw airships rising into the sky. Lots of airships! They are headed this way!"

"Could you tell where they were located?" the Commander asked. "What kind of terrain was there? What color was the sky? Were there buildings?"

The Commander held Tamara's hand to calm her. "Close your eyes and try to recapture the vision. Your attention was focused on the airships. What else could you see?"

"I saw a blue sky. I saw a building emerge from beneath a hill of sand."

"Sand? Not snow?"

Tamara turned frightened eyes to the Commander. "Definitely sand! We are being attacked by Sunan, not Sostor!

And we trusted him! We shared our plans with him! He betrayed us!"

"You don't need my intel. You have the most recent intel of all," praised the Commander, ringing for his aide.

When the aide arrived, the Commander ordered him to activate the entire Security Force. "I'll meet them on the practice field in ten minutes," he directed. "Your Majesty, please come with me." As they hurried to the practice field, the Commander held Tamara's arm and urged her along. "Normally, I would sequester the Head of State in a safe location, but my hunch tells me that you have powers that will save us today. Please stay by my side at all times—and let me know if you have any further visions."

* * * * *

When they reached the practice field, the Commander instructed his aide to activate the "Multiplication Spell," and to ask Solange and Savea to come to the practice field. Tamara looked at him quizzically. "What is that spell?" she asked.

With a strange smile, he answered, "You'll see, Your Majesty." Waving his hand, he opened a hidden door in a wall that led to a series of airlocks. Members of the Security Force lined up at each airlock and proceeded to enter until each airlock was full. The airlocks then closed and the soldiers swam into the ocean beyond. Once the airlocks were empty, they opened onto the practice field to receive new occupants. This process repeated until the practice field was empty.

As Tamara watched, the soldiers shimmered and multiplied until the entire kingdom was surrounded with armed soldiers. "That's amazing!" she cried. "How did you do that?"

The Commander smiled again and told her, "That's a very useful spell, particularly if the odds don't favor you. Now, Your Majesty, please let me escort you through an airlock into the ocean while we await the arrival of the invasion force. The Sisters can join us there."

Tamara and the Commander entered an airlock and walked through into the ocean. Their gills emerged automatically as expected. Looking up, they observed that airships were beginning to appear in the sky above their location. The Commander ordered his troops not to fire until the airships displayed hostile intent. They did not have long to wait.

The first airship fired a rocket toward the undersea Palace. Since the offensive dome had not yet been put in place, Tamara raised her arms in defense and silver rays shot out from her bracelets, vaporizing the rocket.

As other rockets and magical rays were fired from various airships, the soldiers returned fire with mixed results.

The Commander wondered if Tamara could repeat her

original defense with silver vaporizing rays. She mentally responded, *"I tried, but it didn't work."* He looked at her in surprise and thought, *"We can communicate through our minds?"*

"Apparently so," she thought. *"But I don't understand how to activate my powers."*

"Try giving mental commands to your bracelets," suggested the Commander.

Tamara followed his lead and—*"That worked!"* she cried mentally. One by one, she targeted the airships directly and vaporized them. Soon the sky was clear of attack vessels.

"You are a formidable secret weapon!" thought the Commander. *"My hunch was correct."*

Instructing the soldiers to remain on watch, the Commander took Tamara's arm and led her back through the airlock to the practice field. Seeing the Sisters coming toward them, he suggested, "Let's return to my office and check on the Sisters' progress with defenses," he urged. "I'm expecting another attack before long."

Chapter 11
Round Two

Tamara was relaxing on the couch across from the Commander's desk. She kept falling into a state of drowsiness from her defensive efforts a few hours earlier. The Commander closed his office door and pulled up a chair.

Sitting by her, he commented, "I know you're tired, but I want to share a theory with you," he said. "I understand how hard you've been working at trying to understand your powers, but our work together at defeating the first wave of attack has had me thinking. That second crystal on your forehead has been puzzling you. If you try to replay in your memory the first moment out in the ocean when you could link your mind with mine, I believe you will see a connection between that crystal and your newly discovered ability. Remember that you told me that your crystals announce themselves when needed. We needed to be able to communicate out there and we weren't wearing bubble headsets, so I feel confident that your second crystal came to our aid."

Tamara gasped and replied, "I'm certain you are right! Thank you for helping me understand. Do you have any insight into how I might use that ability in the future?"

"You were able to direct the offensive power of your bracelets by mentally asking for it, so I suspect this new power may be accessed in the same way. Why don't you try it right now? I'll stop speaking aloud and only use thoughts," he proposed.

"I'm sending a mental message now," she transmitted. *"Can you hear me?"*

"Loud and clear," he said in his mind, smiling. *"I think this is going to be a very useful connection. Our next experiment will be to communicate this way when others are present to make sure that our messaging is private. I'm going to send for the Sisters."*

*　　*　　*　　*　　*

It wasn't long before Solange and Savea appeared at the door. "What can we do to help, Commander?" asked Solange.

"The Queen and I have discovered at least one feature of the second crystal on her forehead. Let's walk over to the boat and discuss it," he advised.

*　　*　　*　　*　　*

A short time later, they arrived at the boat and the Commander continued his request, "She can link her mind with mine and we can communicate. We would like to perform an experiment with the two of you. Please let us know if you can detect that transmission," explained the Commander.

"How amazing!" cried Savea. "That could be very useful, particularly in battle."

"I agree, Commander," thought Tamara. *"If this communication is truly private, it will be a fantastic benefit"*

"We also need to experiment with how far the communication can extend," added the Commander silently.

"When are you going to transmit to the Commander, Tamara?" asked Solange.

"I already have," admitted Tamara. "And you heard nothing?"

"That's correct," admitted Savea. "Nothing at all. Is it possible to include us in the conversation?"

"I will try. Let's see what happens," thought Tamara.

"Wow!" exclaimed Savea. "I heard that! Solange, did you hear it?"

"I did. How did you do that, Tamara?"

"I focused my thoughts on all three of you—and it seems to have worked!" exclaimed Tamara. *"I wonder how many people could be included?"*

"That's another experiment we must try," promised the Commander, changing to mental communication. *"I would also like to find out whether Tamara can communicate with airships and rockets and perhaps alter their trajectories."*

"That would be beyond useful—it would be a game

changer!" Savea cried.

The aide came running down the path and jumped onto the boat. He ran up to the Commander, who listened carefully to his whispered report.

"It seems that we are about to find out about the crystal's tactical properties. Another wave of airships has been detected. Your Majesty, please accompany me back to the airlock," requested the Commander silently. *"Sisters, please return to your work on defenses and report back to me on your progress. This attack is definitely not over. We are about to engage in Round Two."*

* * * * *

Tamara took the Commander's arm and they hurried to the airlock. Once in the ocean, they looked up to the sky and tried to catch sight of the incoming airships. The Commander mentally asked Tamara to listen telepathically in case she could tune into the inner workings of the ships. She nodded and soon reported, *"Those are 'smart' ships, controlled by magic. There definitely is a consciousness involved. The intent of this assault is to dive to the ocean floor and discharge armed robots."*

"Can you direct them to fly back to their base and self-destruct?" asked the Commander.

"That's a good idea," Tamara replied. *"I'll try."* She raised her bracelets in front of her and sent a silver beam

toward the airships. Slowly, the airships reversed course and headed away from them. In a few minutes, the sky was clear.

"Let's get back to my office," projected the Commander. *"I want to track those airships and see what happens."*

* * * * *

Back in the office, the Commander activated a magical scanner that swept both Mosshire and Mesarra. He frowned and silently said, *"Both kingdoms show no signs of the airships."*

"Then where did they go?" asked Tamara, agreeing to continue their conversation silently.

"My suspicion is that their base is cloaked with invisibility. It may also be shielded with a magical anti-explosion force field or may be underground. When magic is involved, it is very hard to identify such tactics. I was hoping to detect some tremors that might give us a clue, but so far, nothing. The magic must be very powerful," added the Commander.

"I have a 'what if' question," remarked Tamara. *"What if the self-destruct mechanism was not explosive? Could it have been designed to have the robots and ships melt or vaporize? That would be difficult or impossible to detect."*

"That's brilliant!" exclaimed the Commander. *"Of course that would be possible! In my experience, self-destruction has always meant explosion, but that's certainly not an absolute! Prior to the next wave of attack, we need to develop a tracking mechanism that will lead us to that base. I'll get the team right on it."*

"So meanwhile," thought Tamara. *"Where do I go from here?"*

Chapter 12
A New Development

After meeting with the Commander, Tamara felt nervous and without a clear path forward. She decided to return to her bedroom and lie down for a bit. She curled up on her bed and snuggled into the covers. After a few minutes, she was sound asleep.

Entering into a dream state, she found herself flying through clouds. The air surrounding her became gradually colder and she could see that the landscape below was covered with snow. In the distance, she spied a castle protected by a moat. There were many guards protecting the castle, but none of them seemed to be able to see her.

Taking advantage of her apparent invisibility, she flew over the moat and landed in the castle courtyard. She decided to explore and headed for the nearest entrance. Entering the castle, she wandered down the hall, peering into open doorways.

Finding nothing of interest, she ascended a stairway to the second floor. Continuing her search, she came to a door that was closed. Seizing the handle, she discovered that the door was locked. Raising her hands, she directed a silver beam from her bracelets into the lock and heard a click. The door swung open.

There were no lights on in the room, but Tamara could see enough from a small window to identify three seated people. All three were tied to their chairs, which accounted for the lack of guards. Crossing the room, she identified the group as her parents and her sister, Trina.

There was no reaction from any of them, which confirmed Tamara's suspicion that she was still invisible. She decided to try and connect mentally with Trina, who appeared to be quite uncomfortable in her restraints.

"Trina, this is Tamara. Can you hear and understand me?"

Trina's head lifted and she looked around to see where the voice was coming from.

"Yes, I can hear you!" Trina cried. "Where are you?"

Tamara's parents looked over at Trina and asked her who she was talking to.

"I'm talking to Tamara," she replied, "but I can't see her."

"I'm using telepathy, Trina. That's a way we can talk silently with our minds. Ask Father if he can hear me now?"

"He says he can't hear you," answered Trina. "Why is that?"

"I'm guessing it's because he hasn't learned to control his magic," replied Tamara.

"I thought he doesn't have magic," commented Trina.

"He does, and he accessed it one time in defense," thought Tamara.

"Then why can I hear you?" asked Trina.

"I'm guessing that you have almost reached puberty and you are a female descendent of the Super Sisters. You are close to coming into your powers," explained Tamara. *"That's why I have chosen you to be my mental link to the family. Please don't be afraid."*

"I'm not afraid. Can I try sending a thought to you?" asked Trina.

"Sure," responded Tamara.

"This is me, thinking about how much I miss you," thought Trina.

"I hear you!" Tamara sent back. *"That's wonderful! Now we can have private conversations. Are you and our parents okay? Are you hurt in any way? What has been happening to you since you were kidnapped from the Bubble Train?"*

"We're not hurt. We haven't been allowed to do anything or go anywhere. Our captors have been making demands of Father, which he has ignored."

"Can you tell me about your captors? And what demands they are making?" asked Tamara.

"I don't know who they are. And they wear hoods so I can't identify them. Father said the head guy is Sostor, but I don't know what he looks like. I think there's something 'off' about him. He sounds and acts funny. And he keeps trying to make Father sign something."

"Can you ask Father what he is being asked to sign? And does Father also think something is 'off' about Sostor. You're smart and clever."

"I'll try. But where are you? I hear you but I can't see you," Trina complained.

"Actually, I'm in my bedroom. I fell asleep and suddenly was in Mosshire looking for you." responded Tamara. *"Trina, I can feel myself beginning to wake up. I'll return to you if I can..."*

"Tamara, please don't leave me. Tamara...Tamara..."

Tamara sat up abruptly in bed. She had lost contact with Trina. She sent an urgent mental summons to Solange and Savea.

* * * * *

There was a soft knock at the door and Solange entered. "Has something happened, Tamara? Your message was compelling."

"Is Savea with you?" asked Tamara, also suggesting that their conversation be silent.

Complying, Solange said, *"No. She is working on the tunnel to Mosshire. She may be out of range, since we don't know how far your telepathy can reach. Have you also sent for the Commander?"*

"Not yet. I was anxious to see you, but I will now," responded Tamara.

In a few minutes, the Commander joined them. *"Your mental call sounded urgent, Your Majesty," he replied silently. "How can I help?"*

Tamara related how she had fallen asleep and 'flown' to Mosshire. She had found her family and and telepathically communicated with Trina. *"Do you think it was all a dream or was it something more meaningful?"* she asked.

"I can check, Your Majesty," the Commander promised. *"Please permit me to place my hands on your head for a few minutes. I have a spell that can identify mental usage as long as it is employed within a short time."*

"Of course, Commander," agreed Tamara. She sat on her bed and closed her eyes.

The Commander chanted softly and the crystals on Tamara's forehead throbbed in response. In a few minutes, the throbbing subsided and Tamara opened her eyes. *"What did you learn?"* she asked.

"You did drift off into a dream state," the Commander reported. *"But then everything changed. Your crystals took over and actually did transport you a long distance—long enough to reach Mosshire. I don't think your body actually moved; it was more like an astral journey where your spirit does the traveling. I believe your communication with Trina was real and lasted until you tired from the effort and your body awoke. Will you share with us what transpired in your conversation with Trina?"*

Tamara nodded began to do so. When she had finished, both Solange and the Commander were transfixed. *"How amazing!"* Solange exclaimed.

"And Trina felt that something was 'off' about Sostor. That is definitely worth pursuing," offered the Commander. *"Do you think you could repeat that trip to Mosshire?"*

"I don't know," said Tamara. *"But I do know that I would need a good night's rest before trying."*

"There's one more thing we need to talk about," added the Commander.

"And that is?" questioned Tamara.

"When I had my hands on your head, I could feel your crystals. All THREE of them," he emphasized.

"WHAT? I have a third crystal on my forehead?" she

cried.

Solange brushed Tamara's hair aside and affirmed, *"Yes, there are now three on your forehead. My guess is that the first appeared when you needed help with offense; the second, when you needed help with communication and the third when you needed help with an astral journey. Remember how you said the crystals appear when they are needed?"*

"That's right, I did say that." Hugging her grandmother, Tamara climbed into bed and bid her goodnight. The Commander saluted and also left the room, smiling to himself and thinking, *"She is indeed a remarkable woman."*

Chapter 13
From Plan to Action

The next morning, when she awoke, Tamara still felt sleepy and turned over in bed, snuggling deeper into the covers. Slipping once again into a dream state, she found herself once again speeding through the ocean into the air. Soon, she recognized the castle in Mosshire and made her way to the second floor where she had previously discovered her family.

Unlocking the door, she mentally called out to Trina.

"You're back!" responded Trina. *"I'm so glad. I was worried that you wouldn't be able to return."*

"An additional crystal has appeared on my forehead that apparently facilitates such journeys. Have you learned anything about your situation?"

"Yes! I asked Father what Sostor wanted from him and whether he thought Sostor appeared to be 'off'," Trina answered. *"He didn't want to tell me, but I persuaded him. He said Sostor wanted him to abdicate and turn the Kingdom of Marinea over to him. I pointed out that Sostor didn't have any gills, but that seems not to matter. Apparently Sostor has some*

kind of technology that can substitute for gills!"

"Really? What was Father's reaction to Sostor's ridiculous demand?"

"He refused to sign and has ignored Sostor ever since. Sostor is beginning to threaten Mother and me with lifetime imprisonment and possible torture. He really scares me."

"I'm so sorry, Trina, that you have to go through this. Did Father have any comment about Sostor being 'off'?" pursued Tamara.

"He was surprised that I had noticed. But he did agree with me."

"Interesting. Thank you, Trina, for being so observant and persistent. You've been a great help. Please stay alert, and give my love to Mother and Father. We are developing a rescue plan and you need to be able to respond with little or no notice," promised Tamara.

* * * * *

Tamara groaned and sat up in bed. She was fatigued after this second journey and decided that she needed food to regain her strength. She sent a mental request to the Sisters and the Commander to join her at the boat for breakfast and rang for Mia to arrange it.

* * * * *

Walking through the garden toward the boat dock,

Tamara heard footsteps behind her. Turning, she saw the Commander hurrying to catch up with her.

"Good morning, Commander. Thank you for agreeing to join me for breakfast."

"It's my pleasure, Your Majesty," he replied as he tucked her hand through his arm. After walking companionably together, they arrived at the boat and Tamara activated her music device.

"I have a question regarding security, Commander," she began mentally. *"If we are communicating mentally, can't we do so anywhere and be private?"*

"As far as I know, I believe so. That would give us a good deal of flexibility," he agreed. *"We would no longer be restricted to this boat."*

Tamara waved as she spotted the Sisters approaching the boat. *"That would definitely be a benefit,"* she observed.

A breakfast table had already been set for four on the boat deck. As they took their seats and began to enjoy the delicious meal, Solange asked," Do you have news for us, Tamara?"

Tamara nodded and mentally related what had occurred during her second astral journey to Mosshire. *"I believe we need to speed up our rescue plan, given the threats that have been made to my family. How close are we to completing preparations?"*

Savea responded first. *"Are we to communicate mentally? Actually, I think that would be wise. In answer to your question, Solange and I have completed the tunnel to within 100 yards of the Mosshire coast. I put a magical barrier in place to prevent anyone attempting to breach and enter the tunnel from the Mosshire side. When we arrive at that barrier, I can bring it down and finish the tunnel within minutes."*

"That's excellent work," applauded the Commander. *"I commend you. I suggest that Savea and I lead the Security Force through the tunnel at midnight. Hopefully, opposing forces will be minimal at that hour. And Solange, I'd like you to be stationed at the back of the assault force to aid the return to Marinea."*

Both Solange and Savea agreed to the plan, looking to Tamara for approval. Tamara nodded, but added, *"And I will undertake a third astral journey to Mosshire to alert Trina and prepare for rescue. I do not know the extent of my telepathy range, but I will attempt to keep you informed as to my progress. I suspect that my crystals will aid me—they seem to be very good at anticipating my needs!"*

Chapter 14
The Rescue

Just before midnight, the Commander and the Sisters gathered with the Security Force at the entrance to the new tunnel. Everyone was equipped with bubble headgear to facilitate communication.

Savea and the Commander started into the tunnel, followed by the Force, with Solange providing support from the rear. Savea began chanting a spell that would enhance their forward motion.

As they sped along, the Commander asked Savea what she thought of Tamara's new forehead crystal. She shared how amazed she had been to learn of it. She commented that Tamara and the crystals seemed to share a very special bond and wondered if perhaps it was related to the mysterious crystal shards that were shed at the beginning of Creation.

"I don't know," replied the Commander. "The relationship is definitely unique—and certainly very helpful. I don't mean to change the subject, but how close are we to reaching the barrier?"

Savea thought a moment and predicted, "I'd say within just a few minutes. I'll slow us down now so we don't crash into it. When we reach that point, we must maintain silence in case the enemy is on the other side. I'll be able to sense if they are."

The Commander raised his arm and the Force came to a halt. Savea crept up to the barrier and listened for any sound. Hearing none, she waved her hands and vaporized the barrier. Seeing no opposition, she raised her hands again the the tunnel grew ahead of them. Following the newly-created tunnel, they proceeded on toward the Mosshire coast.

Reaching the coast, a small tactical force remained behind with Solange to await the return of the main force. The Commander and Savea led the assault force toward the castle in silent mode.

* * * * *

Meanwhile, Tamara had returned to her bedroom and allowed herself to relax on her bed. Once again slipping into a dream state, she began her journey to Mosshire. Arriving at the castle, she could see the Security Force approaching behind her. She entered the castle and ran up the stairs to her family's room. Unlocking the door, she mentally called out to Trina. Hearing no response, she entered the room to find it empty. Frowning, she considered how to proceed. *"I guess this is where I find out how far my telepathy will reach,"* she thought.

Touching the communication crystal on her forehead,

she focused on trying to reach Trina. Listening carefully, she could detect a weak response from far beneath her. Guessing that the dungeon would be located in that direction, she ran back down the stairs and greeted the Commander.

"I know you can't see me," she projected, *"But my family has been moved, probably to the dungeon below. I'm going down there and I'll report what I find."*

Moving quickly to a staircase, she ran down the steps and reached the dungeon. Trina's voice was louder now and Tamara followed the sound until she arrived at a cell containing her mother and sister. *"Where is Father?"* she asked Trina.

"Sostor took him to a torture chamber. It's in that direction," she gestured to the left. Tamara unlocked the cell holding Trina and her mother and released them, giving each of them a relieved hug. Communicating with the Commander, she described their location and hurried down the hall to locate her father.

* * * * *

Hearing a man's cries just ahead, she increased her speed and arrived at an open cell. Inside, her father was chained to a chair and surrounded by Sostor and several guards. Sostor was yelling, "If you don't do what I want, your wife and daughter will be next in this chamber."

Tamara listened carefully to how Sostor sounded, in

addition to what he was saying. She concluded that his voice had a mechanical quality that she had not heard during his visit to her kingdom. She also noticed that his appearance shimmered slightly and was a bit out of focus. *"He's not real,"* she decided.

Then she turned her attention to her father. Trident was obviously in pain, but his hands were beginning to glow with a blue light. *"His magic is beginning to surface,"* she thought with a smile. *"Father, it's Tamara,"* she projected, *"Your hands are alive with magic. Defend yourself!"*

Trident twisted in the chair and slightly raised his hands. Blue rays shot out and vaporized the guards. When the rays reached Sostor, his image erupted in smoke and disintegrated into a pile of gears and other mechanical remnants. Tamara sent a mental message to the Commander to come and help her.

The Commander was at the cell in a few minutes and proceeded to free the chains holding her father. *"What is that pile on the floor?"* he asked Tamara. *"That is what's left of 'Sostor',"* she replied. *"Clearly, he was not real."*

The Commander identified himself to Trident and assisted him in walking to join his wife and daughter. They met Savea and the Security Force assault team and hurried out of the castle. Reaching the tunnel, they reunited with Solange and the tactical force. As soon as they arrived at the place where the barrier had been, Savea destroyed the piece of tunnel that connected to the coast and reestablished the protective barrier.

When Tamara was certain that her family was safe, she touched her astral journey crystal and found herself once again in her bed. Feeling completely exhausted, she snuggled into her covers and fell asleep.

Chapter 15
Reunion

The next day, Tamara overslept and missed breakfast. When Mia tapped gently at the door, she gladly invited her in. "Did you bring me breakfast?" she asked.

"No, Your Highness. I was going to, but the King told me to wake you and bring you to the Private Dining Room."

Tamara hopped out of bed. As she moved toward her closet, she stopped and turned. "Did you just call me 'Your Highness'?"

"Yes, I did. Did I make a mistake?" asked Mia. "I thought with the King back, you would be a princess again."

"Of course," agreed Tamara. "I didn't think of that. You are right. Please tell the King I will join him as soon as possible."

* * * * *

Entering the Private Dining Room, Tamara was pleased to see that her mother and sister were already present and chatting with her father. Rushing to them, she hugged them to her. "I am so happy to see all of you. I've been worried about your safety," Tamara exclaimed.

"We are so grateful to the new Security Force for

rescuing us," said the King. "That was a very wise move on your part, Tamara. Obviously, you did a very good job as Queen in my absence."

"Thank you, Father," replied Tamara. "When you are ready, we need to brief you on what has occurred since you were kidnapped. And at the same time, I'd like to hear about your experiences in Mosshire."

"Of course," agreed the King. "But let's enjoy a hearty breakfast first."

*   *   *   *   *

When all had eaten their fill, Tamara suggested that they stroll through the garden down to the boat dock. She sent a mental message to the Sisters and the Commander to meet them there.

When everyone had boarded the boat. Tamara activated her music device and distributed bubble headgear to everyone. "Why do we need music and bubble headgear?" asked the King.

"If I may, Your Majesty, please allow me to explain," said the Commander. "We have had to address major security breaches." As the boat proceeded down its track, King Trident was brought up-to-date on the need to protect communications and what had transpired while he was away.

When the Commander had finished his briefing, the

King shook his head and looked lovingly at his family. Solange took his hand and said, "My son, you have been through so much. Are you able to share any of your distress with us?"

"It will be painful, but I believe it is necessary," the King admitted. Holding the hands of his wife and younger daughter, he proceeded to tell a tale of violence, deceit and sadness. "It was so difficult for all three of us," he related. "I was more afraid for Terra and Trina than for myself. Sostor's continued insistence on my abdication was irrational because I knew that the crown would pass to Tamara by law."

"Father, what did you think Sostor was trying to gain?" asked Tamara.

"You," he replied.

"What? Is there something you need to tell me?" prompted Tamara.

"Yes. It wasn't only abdication he was after. He demanded to have you as his wife, thereby cementing his access to our throne."

"That's diabolical!" insisted the Commander.

Savea queried, "Did you detect anything unusual or unexpected about Sostor?"

"Other than his odd behavior?"

"In addition to his odd behavior," Savea clarified.

"Well, all the stress that was building had my head

spinning. Sometimes I had trouble focusing on what he was saying and when I looked at him, he seemed to shimmer around the edges. I didn't know what to make of it," the King explained.

"Father, we believe that the Sostor you saw was not real," said Tamara. "When you were leaving the cell with the Commander, remember that pile of debris on the floor? That was all that remained of the so-called 'Sostor'. It was only an avatar."

"I don't understand," the King replied. "What purpose did such an avatar serve?"

"Misdirection and confusion," responded the Commander. "And that is why we can only discuss serious matters on this boat or through telepathy. Whoever devised this plot must not be allowed to know what we are thinking and planning."

Solange added, "Clearly, someone is trying to gain access to our kingdom and we don't know who or why. Son, is there anything else that you can tell us to help us understand this puzzle?"

"A puzzle of my own," said the King. "All my life, Mother, I have assumed that I was a non-magical. But there were two times during our captivity that my hands glowed and fired blue rays that vaporized the enemy. Can you explain this to me?"

"I believe I can, Son," she offered. "When Sunan was visiting us, he mentioned that power seemed to travel along gender lines." She then explained the mystery of his conception and the theory that one of the Super Brothers was his father. She stressed that the identity of his true father had not as yet been discovered.

"So my father who was ill and subsequently died was also an avatar?" asked the King.

"We have come to that conclusion, Sire," responded the Commander. "It seems that this plot has been a long-standing masquerade."

Crystal Saga

4 - Discoveries

D. E. Weingand

Prologue

My name is Tamara, the former Queen and ruler of the undersea kingdom of Marinea on the planet of Akura. I became ruler suddenly because my father (the King), mother, and younger sister, Trina, were kidnapped from the Bubble Train that they were taking to the mainland kingdom of Alteria. My kingdom needed an interim ruler, and I was next in the line of succession.

I was born with a crystal on my stomach. When I reached the age of puberty, my body added crystals to the palms of my hands and also one to my forehead. Originally, none of us could understand why the crystals appeared or why they suddenly began to change colors, reflecting my emotions. Over time, the capabilities of the crystals became clear. It seems that when I have a need, a crystal emerges to be of assistance.

Our cosmology tells us that in the beginning of Time, the Creator sought to have company and made two Super Beings, one male and one female. Each Super Being wears a powerful crystal in a pendant around the neck.

These Super Beings subsequently created two offspring, one male and one female, each wearing a pendant holding a crystal taken from their Super Being Parents. However, fearing that there would be too much power in just two, the Super Being Parents decided to split each child and their crystal pendant in two, resulting in two male and two female Super Children. The original Super Children wear crystals in golden pendants; their twins wear crystals in silver pendants. When the pendants were created, some crystal shards were left over and a tornado whisked them away. No one knows why or where they were taken.

The two female Super Children, Solange and Savea, reside in my undersea kingdom, which is near several active volcanos. (Solange has a special role: she is my grandmother.) The two males have two separate kingdoms: Sostor in the cold north and Sunan in the warm south.

When I became Queen, we held a reception and invited Sostor and Sunan, as well as friends and dignitaries. It was interesting to watch the two Super Brothers interact. They seemed to be polar opposites, like the lands they inhabit and rule. So far, I have not been able to determine if either of them has hostile intentions toward my kingdom or the Super Sisters, who are my partners in trying to understand my crystals and identifying my related powers.

The Sisters and I have been busy designing strategies for defending the kingdom and ultimately rescuing my family.

I will be forever grateful to the Super Sisters and the Commander of our recently established Security Force (who worked diligently with me to successfully locate and bring my family home).

Once my father was reinstated as King, I returned to being a Princess. It is so wonderful to have my family back, but the political and personal challenges remain. At this point, I am fairly certain that one of the Super Brothers is my grandfather—but which one? We need to uncover the masquerade in order to move forward.

Chapter 1
Home Again

King Trident had retired to his personal quarters after saying good night to his wife and daughters. The rescue effort, although successful, had fatigued him greatly, and he was trying to process all that this day had presented. His mind kept going over the stresses and fears connected to the capture of his family and his failure to protect them.

He also thought about how he had felt when the old king, presumed to be his father, was ill and ultimately died. His connection to the former king had been tenuous at best, and he had trouble bringing up any memory of father-son interaction.

Although he never wanted to leave his family on the mainland, he had felt a strong sense of duty to assume the throne, intending to send for his family once things settled down. However, days flowed into weeks and then into months. Years passed and he had not yet done so. Then the earthquakes struck, and the tsunami swept his house on the mainland away. His wife and two daughters were captured by the waves and nearly drowned. King Trident and his mother, Solange, were able to rescue them and bring them to the undersea kingdom of

Marinea. Tamara, his eldest daughter, had been old enough to have hidden gills that helped her survive, but Terra was from the mainland and Trina was still too young for mature gills. They had been in comas for many days. He had anxiously watched over them as they were nursed back to health, finally reunited as a family.

Once they recovered, the family had little time together as a family before King Trident's royal responsibilities required him to go to the mainland on a state visit. He brought Terra and Trina with him, leaving Tamara behind in charge of the kingdom. Then the kidnapping occurred.

He had so many regrets. His emotions overwhelmed him and he wept. Covering his face with his hands, he suddenly noticed that his hands had a blue glow, just like those two times in Mosshire. Walking to the com unit on the wall, he asked his mother to come to his quarters.

* * * * *

There was a soft knock at his door. He walked over and flung the door open. "Mother! Thank you for coming right over," he cried. Tears started down his cheeks again as he embraced Solange.

"My Son, what is the matter? How can I help you?" murmured Solange. She held Trident closely as he tightened his arms around her. Gently loosening his grip, she walked him over to a nearby couch and sat him down. Clasping his hands, she looked into his eyes and silently chanted a soothing spell.

"Mother, I have been rehashing memories from the time my 'father' died and I claimed the throne until the rescue from Mosshire. I have so many regrets…I have made impossible choices…I just don't know how to fix things. And before you arrived, I was weeping and my hands began to glow blue, just like they did in Mosshire!"

"I will try to guide you through understanding your feelings, Son, if you will allow me," she offered. "You have learned some things in the past few days, but there are other pieces of the puzzle that you have yet to discover."

"Please help me, Mother. I need to understand everything," he pleaded.

"Then I will create a vid screen in front of us so that your memories and mine can also have a visible presence," Solange decided, deftly producing one with an elegant wave of her hands. "The first memory I'll show you is mine, of the night you were conceived. The identity of the masked figure that you see is not known to me. In retrospect, I believe one of the Super Brothers came to me on my wedding night after I had married your so-called grandfather. If my theory is correct, you are the product of two Super Beings. This would mean that your lifelong belief that you are a non-magical is wrong. That blue glow that you have been experiencing is magic trying to emerge—apparently successfully in Mosshire. We can work to release it comfortably."

"Magic? In me?" he exclaimed. "Does that explain why Tamara is so powerful?"

"Indeed it does. You were able to transmit the power you acquired through me when you and Terra conceived her. Also, I believe you can expect Trina to manifest power in some way when she reaches puberty," she added.

"The next vid screen is a kaleidoscope of your childhood. Look it over and let me know if you have any questions," Solange urged.

"Only one," Trident replied. "I don't see myself using any magic. Why is that?"

"I bound your powers when you were a child until you were old enough to use them responsibly. I released them when you came of age—but then you travelled to the mainland, met Terra and fell in love. You remained on the mainland amid a non-magical population until you came to Marinea to assume the throne."

"So I never really had the opportunity to learn or practice. That makes sense. What memory is next?"

"Another kaleidoscope: your early years as king without returning to the mainland."

"I have much regret associated with those years," admitted Trident. "I should have made the effort to connect with my family both on the mainland and also by bringing them here. I was too absorbed in my role and duties as king."

"Let's move on to the next screen. We can come back to regrets," suggested Solange. "This screen is also a kaleidoscope—of the post-earthquake and tsunami time. What memories do you have of that period?"

"I was terrified that my wife and younger daughter would not survive. Yet I was pleased that I could help Tamara adjust to her gills. Her mother had already explained to her that she would one day be able to live beneath the sea. However, when that time arrives, it can be frightening."

"My Son, as you review this time period, please take note that your behavior was loving and nurturing. You did everything you could to help them survive and flourish. I don't see any cause for regret here," reminded Solange. "How are you feeling about it?"

"Actually, while I was afraid for them, I do feel that I did everything possible. And it was wonderful to have them here in my kingdom with me after the tsunami."

"Now we have to turn to the dark period of the kidnapping," Solange determined. "What do you remember of that time and the captivity that followed?"

"Terra, Trina and I were on the Bubble Train heading to the mainland when we suddenly felt cold and found that we were encased in ice," related Trident. "When the train crashed, our ice prison was moved away from the wreckage and we wound up in Mosshire. At first, when the ice was removed, we were given fur robes and treated with hospitality. That didn't last long. Sostor—or what I thought was Sostor—began to make demands and threaten me with harm to Terra and Trina. For some reason, I never questioned Sostor's identity. Looking back, I can see that he was an artificial replica.

"Eventually, the hospitality ended and we were imprisoned in cold cells in the dungeon. I kept refusing Sostor's demands but, at the same time, I was so worried about Terra's and Trina's safety."

"Son, what were those demands exactly?" asked Solange.

"I was asked to abdicate and sign away the kingdom to Sostor. That was part one. Then I was required to sign a marriage contract between Sostor and my daughter, Tamara. I refused both demands repeatedly," he reported. "Next, I was being tortured and we were ultimately rescued by the Security Force."

"During this time, did you ever hear Tamara's voice?" asked Solange.

"I was in so much pain from the torture. I thought I could faintly hear her, but I just assumed it was the pain talking."

"No, she was actually trying to communicate with you." explained Solange. "Her second and third forehead crystals allow her to journey through astral projection and she was nearby, trying to contact you. It was Tamara who found you and gave your position to the Security Force."

"How amazing!" exclaimed Trident. "She is a formidable woman. I'm so proud of her."

"Now let's return to your regrets and what has upset you so much," urged Solange. "If you could rewrite this narrative provided by your memory, what would you change?"

"I would help you figure out the true identity of my father, but that is a project for the future," he replied. "I would still assume the throne since it was my duty to do so. I would make more visits to the mainland to visit my family. I understand why Terra preferred staying there since she is a non-magical and the girls were not yet magical in their pre-teen years. I deeply regret not being more present in their young lives."

"By reviewing all these memories, have you come any closer to seeing a pathway forward?" asked Solange.

"I see three paths at the moment: one would have me

invite my family to remain here with me; a second would have me make more frequent trips to the mainland; and the third would be to abdicate and return to the mainland to be with Terra and Trina, leaving a very capable Tamara as Queen.

"I see the first as problematic since Terra and Trina have lives that are rooted in the mainland. I view the second as an option that could be easily compromised by urgent business requiring me to be in the kingdom. Finally, the third path would lead me away from my duty to succeed my father—but we don't as yet know who that was anyway," complained Trident. "What do you think?"

"There is a fourth path," counseled Solange. "It would involve a modification of the third path in which you would serve as a Special Councilor to the Queen and make trips to Marinea as needed. Your expertise and experience would be valuable."

"That feels perfect!" cried Trident. "I feel very comfortable with that solution. My duty to the kingdom would be fulfilled at the same time as my familial duties. Mother, you are a genius!"

"Don't make a sudden decision," Solange advised. "Give it some thought, talk it over with Tamara, Trina, and Terra. But if you choose that path, I must insist that your frequent visits to Marinea include time with me so that I can assist you with exploring your magic."

Trident put his arms around Solange and held her tightly. "Thank you for your loving guidance, Mother. I will sleep on it and let you know as soon as I choose my path forward."

Chapter 2
The Decision

King Trident considered his decision for many days. He had private sessions with Tamara, Trina, Terra, Solange and Savea where they discussed all four possible pathways. No one could think of any additional choices. They all agreed the final decision would be King Trident's alone.

*   *   *   *   *

One week later, an invitation was circulated around the kingdom. In twenty-four hours, there would be a formal ceremony in the ballroom of the palace, and all citizens were urged to attend. There would be awards and other announcements. Food, beverages, and musical entertainment would be provided.

The kingdom was buzzing with anticipation. What could the king have in mind? Who would be receiving awards? What other announcements might there be? What kind of dress was expected?

*   *   *   *   *

On the day of the ceremony, Tamara asked Solange, Savea, and the Commander to meet her for breakfast in the

Private Dining Room. She specified that all communication would be mental because of security concerns.

When they had seated themselves and ordered food, she opened the conversation by mentally transmitting, "*What do you think Father is up to today*?"

The Commander responded, "*I haven't heard any rumors, which is unusual. I know what physical arrangements are being made, but he seems to be keeping any significant intel solely within his purview*."

The Sisters looked at each other and agreed that they had not learned anything of significance either. But Solange mentioned that her son had requested that she wear formal attire and to let others know his wishes as well.

"*That's useful information*," thought Tamara. "*He must have something really special planned. I wonder if he has made a decision?*"

After enjoying their breakfast, they separated in order to change clothes for the ceremony.

* * * * *

At the appointed time, the ballroom doors swung open, and an excited crowd filed in. At the far end of the room, King Trident sat upon his throne, flanked by his family, the Sisters and the Commander. Tamara had brought her music device in order to partially scramble the sound.

The king stood and welcomed everyone, thanking them for honoring his invitation. He gave a brief apology for his recent absence, characterizing it as an unanticipated trip abroad.

He then asked the Commander to join him, introducing him to the population and praising his efforts at improving conditions in the kingdom. Placing a ribboned medal over the Commander's head, he acknowledged the importance of the new Security Force and authorized similar medals for the members involved in recent security efforts. Bowing, the Commander thanked him on behalf of his entire Force and stepped back to his previous position on the dais.

"Would the Sisters please join me?" asked the King.

Solange and Savea did as the king requested and stood before him. He took two more medals and draped them around their necks, thanking them profusely for their service. He hugged them and said, "I am so lucky to have a mother and aunt who are so loving and powerful. You have my eternal gratitude."

After the Sisters returned to the dais, the king led the citizens in enthusiastic applause. Then he turned to the audience and commented, "During my travels and over many days, I have been evaluating my life choices," he began. "I have made some decisions in order to improve my life and for the good of the kingdom."

The citizens looked around, puzzled. A buzz of whispered questions rose from them. The leader of the king's councillors stepped forward and asked, "What exactly are you proposing, Sire?"

"I have thought long and hard about my options," he replied. "While I have consulted trusted advisors, the decisions are mine alone. Therefore, I propose the following:

- I shall abdicate my role as king to focus on my roles as husband and father. Princess Tamara did an exceptional job as queen regent during my absence. As she is next in the line of succession, she shall assume the throne and the title of Queen of Marinea, if she will accept.

- I will ask the Queen to appoint me as Senior Councilor.

- I will relocate, with my wife and younger daughter, to the mainland and make regular trips back to Marinea as needed or wanted.

- I request, with her and the Queen's approval, that my mother, Solange, spend six months of the year in Marinea as Senior Advisor to the Queen and six months with me and the rest of my family on the mainland.

- I also request, with her and the Queen's approval, that my Aunt Savea also be appointed a Senior Advisor to the Queen.

The ballroom fell silent. There was not even a whisper. Then a smattering of applause grew in volume until everyone was clapping merrily. Members of the king's Council looked at each other in relief, pleased that the king would retain a connection to the administration of the kingdom.

Tamara walked forward to receive the crown and scepter and stood by her father. "Your Majesty and Father, I fully support your desires and wish you well going forward. I am pleased that you have decided to continue sharing your experience with us and look forward to ongoing communication with you, whether you're here or afar." She kissed his cheek and hugged him close. "When will you be leaving for the mainland?"

"We have affairs of state to discuss in order to make this a seamless transition. When that has been accomplished, I will make travel plans," the ex-king replied. Turning to his wife and younger daughter, he inquired, "I hope these proposals are acceptable to you both?"

Terra and Trina hugged him with tears in their eyes.

"Oh, Father, I am so happy," cried Trina.

"It will be so wonderful to have you home again," Terra smiled.

Tamara joined her family to celebrate the new future that beckoned them. Waving to the Commander, she invited him to accompany her as she walked toward the food and drink that looked so tempting. "*I think that went well,*" she thought. "*Do you agree*?"

"*I do,*" he replied. "*It's a win/win solution for almost everybody—except you.*"

"*What do you mean*?" Tamara asked mentally.

"*The weight of the kingdom is now permanently on your shoulders. Before, you were Queen temporarily, until we devised a successful rescue plan. Have you absorbed the impact of what has just happened?*" he wanted to know.

"*Intellectually, yes. Emotionally, probably not,*" she responded. Placing her hand on his arm, she looked at his face, "*I hope you will continue to be in my corner.*"

Covering her hand with his, he promised that he would.

Chapter 3
Moving Forward

The next morning, Tamara lay in bed pondering the future. The Commander was right—she had seen herself as an interim queen. Yet she totally agreed with her father's decision. The entire family would prosper under the new arrangement. It would be up to her to assure that the kingdom would also thrive.

As she dressed for the day, she decided that the first order of business would be a meeting with the Council. Any fears or worries that the councilors had would need to be addressed. Then the meetings with her father would begin so that the official transfer of power would be seamless.

Always in the back of her mind lurked the unanswered questions as to the identity of her true grandfather and the perpetrators of her family's kidnapping. As she dressed for the day, her mind kept churning. She decided that a third meeting needed to be added to her day: a problem-solving session with the Commander, Solange, and Savea. Those unanswered questions shouldn't be placed on the back burner. She had a hunch that they would affect everything else on her agenda.

*   *   *   *   *

The meeting with the Council went smoothly. She had been somewhat apprehensive, but her recent performance as Queen had paved the way for a solid working relationship. She looked forward to positive interactions with the Council members. After responding to their questions and allaying a few expressed fears, she scheduled a date for their next meeting and moved on to the second appointment on her schedule.

Next was the first meeting with her father as the prior head of state. Outranking her father was a new experience and she tried her best to tread lightly. She was impressed with what he had to share and the ease with which he revealed both challenges and successes. It was apparent that he had been an excellent king and that the handoff of power would be very straightforward. At the conclusion of the meeting, she hugged her father and complimented him on his tenure as king and his willingness to entrust her with the future of the kingdom.

Before her third and final appointment, she headed to the Private Dining Room for a nourishing lunch to replenish her energy. As she scanned the menu to decide what to order, the Commander stopped by her table and asked if he could join her. Pleased, she motioned him to the chair beside her.

"Good day, Commander," she said with a smile, while gesturing that communication should be silent. The

Commander nodded in agreement.

"*How did your morning meetings go*?" he asked.

"*I think quite well,*" she answered. "*The Council and I seem to be ready to collaborate in governing the kingdom. I have scheduled another meeting with them. And I am so pleased with how my father and I could work together in the transfer of power. My main concern is this afternoon's problem-solving session. I don't know what direction to take.*"

"*None of us do,*" commented the Commander. "*It's undoubtedly going to be mostly brainstorming. By the way, in informal situations—like lunch—would you be willing to use my first name instead of my title?*"

"*That seems reasonable,*" Tamara replied. "*And you may do the same. What is your name*?"

"*I was named after my grandfather, Sean.*" he explained. "*He was also a soldier, but had no known magical skills. My abilities in that area can be traced to an uncle on my father's side. My father died young so I don't know if he had magic or not.*"

"*Then Sean it is,*" Tamara smiled. "*My knowledge of the genealogy of magic is limited, but my understanding is that it follows gender lines. I've learned that my father's magic was bound by my grandmother until he was old enough to handle it responsibly—but then he decided to travel to the mainland, where he met my mother, and his magic was never fully developed. I believe my grandmother intends to help him with that when she visits him.*"

"*So you think my grandfather may have had latent magic that was never released?*" he asked.

"*I think that may be possible,*" Tamara replied. "*Another mystery to be investigated?*"

"*At some point, perhaps,*" he mused. "*It's not at the top of the mystery pile, though.*"

They continued to mentally chat companionably while they enjoyed their lunch. Before long, the time arrived when they needed to move on to the problem-solving session. Rising, Tamara led the way into the garden and down the path to the boat.

* * * * *

Solange and Savea were already on the boat when they arrived. Activating her music device, Tamara invited everyone to be seated. "*I brought the sound dampening device because, although we will be mentally communicating, I wanted to add another layer of safety. This committee must operate within an atmosphere of utmost secrecy.*"

Solange nodded agreement. "*What we discuss here will have far-reaching implications. Tamara, did your morning meetings go well?*"

"*Very well,*" answered Tamara. "*I'd like to start our conversation with a request. Grandmother, would you be willing to accompany my family on their journey to the mainland? Since we agree that one of the Super Brothers came to your room on your wedding night, it is possible that the same individual was involved with the kidnapping. I would feel more comfortable if you, as another Super Being, would be with them as protector since my father's magic is as yet unformed.*"

"*I think that's an excellent idea,*" seconded the Commander. "*We need to provide maximum protection.*"

Solange asked whether their telepathic communication could extend all the way to the mainland. "*I have confidence that it will, Grandmother,*" Tamara replied. "*During the rescue, I was able to use it over long distances without difficulty. If it turns out that the range is limited, my crystals have never let me down and I think they will increase the range.*"

"*With that assurance, I will gladly accompany them,*" agreed Solange. "*While I am on the mainland with Trident, I will help him learn to use his magic.*"

"*I was hoping you would do so,*" said Tamara. "*You have helped me so much.*"

"*Do we have any new intel on the identities of the perpetrators of these crimes against our kingdom*?" asked

Savea.

"*Nothing solid,*" replied the Commander. "*But I have suspicions and would like to increase surveillance on both Brothers.*"

"*How would you do that?*" inquired Tamara.

"*In my magical studies, I used to tinker with making magical birds. I could design some birds that are appropriate to the two climates and have them fly random patterns above the two kingdoms. If I do say so, my birds were very realistic!*" bragged the Commander.

Tamara clapped her hands and commented, "*That's a great idea! Please get started right away!*"

"*Savea, have you learned anything new?*" asked Solange.

"*There have been efforts on the Mosshire end of the tunnel to bore through the barrier. Although I destroyed the tunnel's extension to the coast, I detected magic repairing it and it is back in place. I plan to eliminate the entire tunnel tomorrow,*" Savea promised.

"*How will you do that?*" inquired the Commander.

"*It was my magic that created it, so I can easily take it out,*" she answered.

"*Let me help you with that,*" offered Solange. "*Why don't we disconnect it at our end and loop the tunnel back to*

Mosshire? That way, when they breach the barrier and travel through the tunnel, they will wind up back at Mosshire!"

Savea hugged her sister. "*What a marvelously devious idea*!"

Tamara and the Commander looked at each other and started laughing. "*Well, since everybody but me has an 'assignment'*," summarized Tamara, "*I will focus on taking a daily relaxing 'nap' so that my crystals can monitor what is taking place on the ground in the two kingdoms. With birds in the air and my crystals alert to ground activities, we should have a pretty good handle on surveillance. Let's meet here again tomorrow to share our progress.*"

Heading back to the palace, the Commander tucked Tamara's hand through his arm. The Sisters looked at each other and smiled.

Chapter 4
The Next Day

The Commander sent a mental invitation to Tamara to come to his office to inspect the prototypes of his magical birds. Excitedly, Tamara hurried over to his office.

"*Come in, come in,*" the Commander urged. Taking her hand, he led her behind his desk and pressed a small panel. The wall slid open, revealing a spacious laboratory. "*This is my workroom where I experiment with magical ideas*." Walking over to a table, he proudly showed her the prototypes he had created.

Picking up a white bird, he explained, "*This is a Tundra Swan. It prefers very cold habitats, so it is perfect for Mosshire. This other one is a Royal Tern, common to hot and dry climates like Mesarra. What do you think*?"

"*They're beautiful. But how do they function*?" she asked.

"*Watch those vid screens along the far wall.*" He picked up the swan and waved it around the room. Images of the room appeared on the left vid screen.

"*Fascinating,*" Tamara praised. "*You have created a*

marvelous surveillance tool! When will these birds be operational—and how do we get them to their target locations?"

"*They are operational now. I just have to make more of them so there are enough to cover the areas. I need a few days,*" he responded.

"*That's perfect,*" she replied. "*Now I'm going to take one of my relaxing 'naps' to see if I find any intel that might be useful to you.*"

The Commander took her hand and kissed it. "*Thank you for believing in me.*" She blushed and hurried from his workroom.

*   *   *   *   *

Tamara opened the door to her bedroom and walked quickly to her bed. Curling up in the covers, she relived the moment when Sean had kissed her hand. The memory was so delicious that she almost blushed again. She wondered if she would be able to relax enough to summon any visions. Her attention was focused squarely on that kiss, and she brought her hand to her lips. "*He really is a handsome man,*" she thought. "*So charismatic and competent in magical skills. I wonder what it would be like if he really kissed me…*" and she drifted off to sleep.

She felt herself flying again, but this time the

landscape was different. Instead of snow, she could see piles of sand. "*This must be Mesarra*," she thought. "*I wonder what is drawing me to Sunan?*"

A large building came into view, which she guessed was a palace. Entering the front door, she passed large groups of guards who obviously could not see her. Moving further down the hall, she stopped at a closed door from which she heard loud voices shouting. She wondered if she could enter the room without opening the door and decided to try. In a moment, she was inside the room staring at both Super Brothers.

Sostor was seated on a chair, but he didn't seem able to move. Surely magic was being used to hold him fast. Sunan paced back and forth, screaming "We had a deal, Brother. You were to kidnap King Trident and his family and force his abdication. I was to play nice with Tamara and try to woo her. I was succeeding on my end, and then you decided to bow out."

"I had never met Trident and his family before," retorted Sostor. "I was stunned at how much he resembled me. Think back to that crazy plan you cooked up with avatars and robots. I was willing to participate because I was intrigued with the idea of making love to Solange—which was delightful, by the way. But you never told me that I left her with child. Once I saw Trident, I knew."

"*Whoa*!" thought Tamara. "*That solves several of our*

mysteries!"

"And you didn't expect me to find out that you were going to return them to Marinea?" yelled Sunan.

"No. I hoped you would be so involved with your plotting that you wouldn't notice until it was too late," answered Sostor.

"Well, Brother, it's a good thing I didn't trust you. I had contingency plans in place. As you are now aware, I had developed an artificial clone of you that was ready to step in if, as was necessary, I had to remove you from Mosshire," ranted Sunan.

"So now what, Brother?" asked Sostor. "Are you going to try and kill me? Do you realize that if you succeed, you will die as well?"

Tamara felt her energy waning and knew that she had to wake up her body. She clasped her bracelets and focused on her bedroom. Gasping, she sat upright in her bed. She sent an urgent telepathic message to the Commander, Solange and Savea to meet her immediately at the boat.

Chapter 5
Questions Have Answers

Tamara washed her face and grabbed a sweater. She practically raced down the path to the boat. The boat deck appeared to be empty. She hoped that the others would arrive soon and activated her music device. Hearing a noise from inside the cabin, she spun to see the Commander emerge.

"*I hit the jackpot*!" she cried. "*I have the answers to many of our questions!*"

When they were seated, he put his arm around her, and her head naturally leaned on his shoulder. As he kissed her forehead, he spotted the Sisters heading toward them. Standing, he saluted and welcomed them aboard.

Solange and Savea chose seats near them and looked at a flustered Tamara. "*What has happened*?" asked Savea.

Tamara took a deep breath and began, "*I went on another astral journey and it took me to Mesarra. I'll give you the highlights and then we can discuss the details. First of all, Sunan was holding Sostor prisoner using some type of magic. They were having a very loud argument. I learned that Sostor was your visitor on your wedding night, Grandmother. He was part of a plot that both Brothers shared. He fondly remembers that night, but he never knew that he had fathered a child until he met father during the kidnapping and saw the resemblance.*

"However, they planned that Sunan was to woo me and he felt like he was succeeding. Back at Mosshire, Sostor was preparing to return my family to Marinea, and Sunan found out. Sunan left here so suddenly because he had learned of Sostor's defection. By the way, all those artificial beings we encountered were created by Sunan. I felt my energy being depleted so I asked my bracelets to return me to my bed. Then I sent a telepathic call to all of you. Now we can discuss details."

The Sisters and the Commander stared open-mouthed as Tamara related her tale. "*If those were the highlights, I can hardly wait to hear the details!*" shared Savea.

For the next two hours, they peppered Tamara with questions and tried to thoroughly debrief her. At the conclusion of their conversation, they looked at each other in amazement. So many questions now had answers.

In addition, the Commander informed them that his birds had been deployed that morning and would be sending back images within the day.

"*How did you manage to get them ready so fast?*" asked Tamara. "*I thought it would take a few days.*"

"*I knew it was urgent so I didn't go to sleep last night,*" he responded. "*Now we need to figure out a path forward.*"

"*One more thing,*" interrupted Tamara. "*I also heard Sostor ask Sunan if he was going to kill him, and he reminded him that if he did, he would die, too.*"

"*That is true,*" admitted Solange. "*Since we twins came from single beings, if one dies, the other does also.*"

"*I wish I could have waited to hear Sunan's response, but my energy was too low,*" complained Tamara.

"*You did amazingly well, Tamara,*" praised Savea. "*We know so much now, and there are fewer blanks to fill in.*"

"*Grandmother, how do you feel now that you know who was with you on your wedding night? Sostor apparently agreed to the plan because he was attracted to you,*" added Tamara.

"*It will take me some time to process this. We certainly had the Brothers pegged wrongly,*" responded Solange. "*Commander, from a tactical point of view, what do you think Sunan will try next?*"

"*Well, he doesn't know what we have discovered, and that's a good thing. I suspect my birds will provide some clues over the next few days. If I were in his position and I knew that killing my twin would be tantamount to suicide for me, I would put him in a secure prison,*" decided the Commander.

"*And such a prison would need to be magically*

enhanced, wouldn't it?" asked Tamara.

"*Definitely*," he agreed. "*Fortunately, my magical birds are able to detect where magic resides. We should be able to locate Sostor easily when we are ready to do so. Your Majesty, I am going to check on the birds now. Would you like to accompany me*?"

"*Yes, I would. Those birds fascinate me,*" she added. "*And then I need to rest. It's been quite an eventful day.*"

When they were alone, Solange and Savea sat down once again to share what was on their minds. Savea reminded Solange that they needed to mentally communicate since the music device had left with Tamara.

Savea teased, "*So Sostor had a 'thing' for you? Was he a good lover?*"

"*I already told you that I enjoyed the evening*," admitted Solange. "*But it has been difficult all these years, not knowing who Trident's father was.*"

"*Now that you do know…*"

"*It's much too soon to make any judgments*," Solange asserted. "*There are many game pieces still on the board. Time will tell…*"

Chapter 6
Birds in Flight

When the Commander and Tamara reached his office, he asked if she was too tired to proceed and offered to wait until the next day to check on the birds.

"*I am tired,*" she admitted, "*But I'm also curious. Let's try, and I'll let you know if I need to rest.*"

They went behind the desk and the Commander pressed the entry pad. When the wall slid open, he took Tamara's hand and they walked into the workshop. As the opening slid closed behind them, he pointed to the wall of screens. "*What you see on the left side is in real time. The screens on the right will show selected still images from the past 24 hours,*" he explained.

Tamara examined the left side first and did not detect anything of particular interest. However, when she moved to the right side, she exclaimed, "*Look at that! Sostor has indeed been moved into a cell, and the birds captured it because it is magically enhanced. And over here, there seems to be a courtyard full of robots outfitted for battle. Since the birds also targeted that, doesn't it mean that magic is in play there as well?"*

"*Definitely,*" agreed the Commander. "*I would interpret this scene as a prelude to an attack. Now we have to determine how and when it will take place so we can prepare for it.*"

"*I need to rest now so that I can make another astral journey,*" said Tamara. The Commander led her out of the workroom and walked her to her bedroom. "*I will have some refreshments brought so you can re-energize when you awaken,*" he promised and kissed her on the cheek. Flushing, she entered her room and hurried to her bed. She was asleep as soon as her head hit the pillow.

While she was sleeping, the Commander returned to his workshop to make a record of the time stamps on the selected screens. He was shocked to note that the shots had been taken hours ago. That meant that an attack could already be underway! He examined the courtyard shot again. Those piles against the wall were not of sand—they were made of snow! The attack would be coming from Mosshire! He needed to find the Sisters immediately. He sent them a mental message to meet him at the boat as soon as possible!

* * * * *

Tamara tossed and turned. She wondered if she had slept and, if so, for how long. She was still so tired. Her bracelets began to glow, lighting up the entire room. Suddenly, she was on the boat! She wondered if she was dreaming or doing an astral projection, but no—she was actually on the boat!

She saw the Commander running to the boat. Greeting him, she asked if anything was wrong. He told her about the connection to Mosshire and that the attack would be coming from there.

"*That's awful,*" she cried. "*The Sisters are in the tunnel working on dismantling it. Are they in danger?*"

"*I'm afraid so,*" he replied. "*I sent them a mental message to meet me here and they haven't responded. Why are you here? How did you get here?*"

"*My bracelets have shown me a new power: they teleported me here,*" she answered. "*Please activate the Security Force and meet me in the tunnel. I'm going to teleport to their location.*" She turned and was gone.

* * * * *

While the Commander was following Tamara's orders, she instantly found herself in the tunnel next to the Sisters. Savea was alarmed when Tamara suddenly appeared. Solange was only a little less surprised. "*How did you get here*?" they asked together.

Tamara briefly described her bracelets' new power and alerted them to the imminent invasion. "How far have you progressed with disabling the tunnel?" she inquired. Upon hearing that they had only just begun, she proposed that they sever the tunnel where they were standing. "*Since the coming attack force is composed of robots, I'm hoping the salt water of the ocean will deactivate them. However, they are carrying magic in some form, so we may be the line of first defense. The Commander is bringing the Security Force as I speak. Now, how can I help*?"

The women combined their magic to sever the tunnel Salt water pour into the tunnel in both directions. Savea had an idea and diverted lava from a nearby volcano into the segment of the tunnel leading to Mosshire. Solange sealed the tunnel on their end so that the lava could not flow back toward them.

Within a few minutes, the Commander appeared with the Security Force. Looking around, he was amazed at what the women had already accomplished. "*I have diverted some of the birds to follow the attack force*," he reported. "*I can report that the lava has totally covered them and they are immobile. I will leave some men here to monitor the area and make sure their magic does not resurrect them!*"

Turning to Tamara, he asked if she would like to teleport back to her bed or take the long way by walking. Smiling, she took his arm and indicated that a walk would be lovely.

Chapter 7
What's Next?

Tamara sat with the Commander on a bench in the garden. No one could overhear their conversation, as they maintained their mental connection. Tamara's skirt conveniently covered the fact that they were holding hands.

Tamara spoke first, "*Hopefully, we have repelled the first salvo. But have you any idea what Sunan may be planning*?"

"*I have to think like an amoral dictator*," Sean replied. "*I think he is aiming at world domination. He has his kingdom, he has the ruler of Mosshire, and all he needs is you.*"

Tamara shuddered, then offered, "*Well, if he needs me, that's not going to happen.*"

"*But what if he threatens your family? What would you do to save them*?" asked Sean.

"*I would fight*!" asserted Tamara, squeezing Sean's hand. Sean turned toward her and kissed her lips gently. "*I will always be at your side*," he promised.

*　　*　　*　　*　　*

No sooner had the Commander returned to his office

than he received an urgent communication from the guards he had left watching the tunnel. They alerted him to visible movement beneath the lava layer covering the robots. He ordered them to continue monitoring the scene, but to retreat to a safe distance. Then he sent additional troops to reinforce the guards. Finally, he sent a mental message to Savea to join him in the tunnel.

It came as no surprise to him when he met Savea to find Tamara already there. It appeared that her bracelets were also on watch and teleported her to the tunnel as soon as it was deemed necessary. However, she was no longer dressed as a queen. Instead, she wore body armor that allowed her crystals free range of motion.

Savea was also in body armor and looked ready for battle. She asked the Commander what kind of magic could allow the robots to free themselves from the lava. He answered that it was called a "resurrection" spell, only available to the most powerful of sorcerers. "*We need to plan carefully how to merge our magic if we are going to be able to defeat that level of sorcery,*" he stressed. "*As we have observed in the past, it is likely that Tamara will be the wild card enabling us to be successful.*"

"*What do you think about this idea*?" Savea offered. "*I can turn the lava flow to cover the robots once again—and then*

I can cause a landslide that is quite deep to add weight to that lava layer."

"*Let me add one more deterrent,*" suggested Tamara. "*I can solidify your work with an immobility spell which should keep them from breaking through.*"

"*We can try it,*" agreed the Commander, "*But let's keep brainstorming in case that resurrection spell is able to overcome what we've planned.*"

"*Uh oh,*" the Commander sighed, "*My aide has just messaged me that we can expect an air assault that is almost upon us. I'm puzzled. If Sunan needs you as his bride, Tamara, why is he continuing to attack with weapons that are capable of killing you?*"

"*Probably because my death would make the kingdom confused and vulnerable. My father would need to return to the throne, as the line of succession ends with me,*" she explained. "*No, wait! Could the line of succession also include Solange, as father's mother? Perhaps he is trying to eliminate her as well.*"

"*And if he were successful,*" added Savea, "*Remember that I would die, too.*"

"*True,*" appraised the Commander. "*What a cruel and barbaric strategy.*"

"*Savea, is the double dome completed over the*

kingdom?" asked Tamara.

"*Yes*," Savea replied. "*But what if it doesn't hold*?"

"*It's true that we are dealing with a master sorcerer*," affirmed the Commander. "*But Savea, you are an equally powerful Super Being. What do you suggest that we do?*"

"*I'm sending a message to Solange. We need her here*," stressed Savea.

* * * * *

It was only a few minutes before Solange joined them in the tunnel. "*What is happening*?" she asked. Savea related what they had found out about the resurrection spell and the ongoing attempt of the robots to break free of the lava. The Commander added his belief that Sunan was the master sorcerer responsible for the spell, but that either Sister was equally powerful and could defeat him.

Tamara's bracelets began to glow. She clasped the Sisters' hands and a golden haze surrounded them. When the haze lifted, the Sisters had merged into one being. Stretching out their arms toward the end of the tunnel, they sent a bolt of lightning at the pile of lava and the robotic arms reaching from it. There was an explosion and the entire pile, with the robots inside, had vaporized. Tamara grasped their hands again and the Sisters became their original two selves.

"*What did you just do*?" asked the Commander.

"*It wasn't my idea,*" she replied, "*My bracelets prompted my actions. I believe it is possible that Sunan has managed to drain power from Sostor and only a united female Super Being could outperform him. He must be pretty annoyed now!*"

"*What about the air assault*?" asked Solange.

"*Savea thinks the double dome will hold, but I'll return to the palace and monitor it,*" promised Tamara.

"*I'm afraid I must ask your father to postpone his trip to the mainland with your mother and sister. I think we're going to need all hands on deck until this emergency is resolved. Solange, would you please begin his magic training immediately*?" the Commander requested.

"*Of course,*" she promised. "*When he is comfortable with his magic, I think he will be an asset to our team.*"

Chapter 8
Trident Joins the Team

Solange knocked on the door of Trident's quarters. When he answered, she asked him to accompany her to the boat, where she activated the music device that she had borrowed from Tamara and handed him a bubble headset.

Once their conversation was private, she apprised him of all that had happened the previous day at the rescue tunnel. He looked shocked and yet proud of what Tamara had accomplished. Solange impressed upon him what the Commander had advised, that the trip to the mainland needed to be postponed.

"So, my Son," continued Solange, "It is imperative that your magic lessons begin immediately. We will need you in the coming weeks to help us defend the kingdom.

"What can you remember about the three times you used magic? Think about your emotions, your intents, and anything else—whether it seems relevant or not."

Trident thought for a moment and then shrugged, "I really didn't have any intent. I was surprised when my hands started to glow. My emotions were complex: fear, anger, revenge, and trying to protect my family."

"What made you raise your hands in front of you?" asked his mother.

"It just seemed like the thing to do," he replied. "Instinct?"

"Now that we know who your father is, the fact that you have magic is no surprise. Your parents are both Super Beings, so our offspring would be a powerful sorcerer. Since your magic has been lying dormant for so many years, it needs to be accepted by you and then trained," Solange instructed.

Trident nodded and agreed to do whatever his mother suggested.

*　　*　　*　　*　　*

Tamara stopped at her father's door and knocked. "*Come in,*" her grandmother answered. "*We've been evaluating your father's magical instincts*."

"*I need to ask both of you to follow me,*" insisted Tamara. "*An air assault is imminent and I would appreciate reinforcements.*"

"You two seem like you're talking, but I don't hear anything," complained Trident.

"Father, listen with your mind," prompted Tamara. "*Use your magic. Can you hear me now*?"

"*Yes! That's amazing!*" Trident exclaimed. "*What do*

you call it?"

"It's telepathy. My bracelets have enabled that magical skill for all of us. Our Security Force has discovered many listening devices around the palace, so we needed to be able to communicate without talking. Please use it when you are anywhere other than the boat," insisted Tamara. *"Let's go out into the garden so we can observe the double dome over the kingdom. We need to know if it will repel the air assault."*

* * * * *

Once in the garden, they selected a bench with a clear view of the sky. Before long, there were shadows moving above the domes. One by one, they dropped what looked like some type of missiles, although the domes prevented a clear view. The projectiles struck the outer dome and self-destructed. The outer dome did not appear damaged. However, the assault had triggered it to take action and it fired at the missile-carrying shadows until they exploded in flames. Several minutes later, the sky was clear and the assault appeared to be over.

The Commander joined them and warned that a second wave of assault was coming soon. As they kept watch, Tamara asked Trident how the "magic lessons" were coming along. He sighed and told her that his magic was apparently tied to his emotions, and there were no emotional impulses connected to lessons. "*Emotions, eh? Just like the colors of my crystals and my hair. We must be related!*" she joked. "*Don't worry, Father. Your emotions will trigger the magic when the time is right.*"

"*This telepathy is so convenient,*" he approved. "*Your bracelets are a wonder.*"

"*Invasion alert*!" cried the Commander. "*Be ready.*"

The second wave of attack involved small globes dropped at random across the domes. They splashed easily through the ocean water above the domes and exploded when they struck the surface of the domes. The outer dome began to develop cracks. Tamara shouted, "Seal the cracks!" as she directed beams from her bracelets upward. Trident also raised his arms, and blue rays shot upward, repairing the cracks. Solange took a different approach: She aimed for the airships high above the ocean and sent a wave of energy skyward that took out most of them. The few that remained turned and flew away.

"*That was a very effective defense. Congratulations everyone,*" applauded the Commander. "*I'm not aware of a third attack wave, but we must remain vigilant.*"

Chapter 9
Correcting an Imbalance

The next day, Savea knocked on the Commander's office door. "*Those first two waves of attack were impressive,*" she said. "*Do you have any intel that I should be aware of?*"

"*I do not,*" he responded, "*And that worries me.*"

"*What about the birds?*" she asked. "*What are they transmitting?*"

"*Everything looks normal and peaceful,*" he replied. "*I think it's time for Tamara to take another 'relaxing' nap.*"

"*She's just finishing breakfast,*" Savea said. "*I'll let her know.*"

Leaving his office, she found Tamara walking toward her bedroom. Savea informed her of the Commander's concerns and recommendation. Tamara nodded in agreement and entered her bedroom. Savea followed, intending to sit by her bed.

"I'll be here in case you need me," Savea promised. "But I want you to remember something. When you helped Solange and me resolve our differences, you noticed that there was an imbalance between us. At the time, we wondered if the male Super Beings also had one. It could be a factor as you

take your astral journey."

"*I'll watch for it,*" murmured Tamara as drowsiness began to overtake her. Within minutes, she was once again on her way to find Sunan and Sostor. Finding herself in the palace dungeon, she easily located Sostor's cell. Peering inside, she saw Sostor sitting on the edge of an uncomfortable looking cot. Drifting inside the cell, she stood before him and mentally called out, "*Grandfather.*"

Sostor looked up and searched with his eyes around the cell. "*Who calls me*?" he silently asked. Tamara thought to herself, "*He hears me. That's helpful.*"

"*It's me, Grandfather: Tamara,*" she answered. "*We have a mental connection.*"

"*Where are you, Tamara*?" he asked.

"*My spirit is in your cell with you,*" she responded.

"*How is that possible*?"

"*My crystals have enabled me to visit you,*" she explained. "*How are you, and do you have access to your magic*?"

"*As you can see, I am a prisoner. Sunan has drained me of much of my magic, but he knows better than to take it all or I would die and then he would also.*"

"*Does Sunan ever come inside your cell*?"

"*Sometimes—to check on my magic level. He wants to*

make sure that I haven't figured out how to build it up again."

Tamara put her astral hand on Sostor's arm and asked, "*Can you feel that*?"

"*Very faintly, but it's nice to know that you are here.*"

"*When Sunan comes, does he touch you? Or can you touch him*?" she asked.

"*In order to gauge my magic, he does need to touch me. Why*?"

"*You'll see. I'm going to send you some of my magic now, and hopefully he will notice.*"

* * * * *

Tamara heard footsteps running down the hall and stopping at the cell. Sunan unlocked the cell door and rushed in, leaving guards stationed just outside. "What's going on here?" he demanded. "My sensors have detected an influx of magic!"

"I don't think that's possible, Brother. You have taken most of my magic from me," complained Sostor.

Sunan brought a cuff that looked like one designed to take blood pressure and placed it around Sostor's upper right arm. As he adjusted it, Tamara sent a golden haze from her bracelets that surrounded both Brothers. Slowly, the two Brothers merged into one entity that rose into the air and revolved. After a short time, the golden haze dissipated—just as it had done with the Sisters—releasing the single entity to the cot and dividing it once again into the two Brothers.

Tamara could no longer detect an imbalance. Exhausted, she could feel her energy depleting, and she was pulled back into her sleeping body. Savea was watching her intently. In a short while, Tamara awoke and Savea asked what she had learned.

"*I was able to mentally communicate with Grandfather and infuse some of my magic into him. That was detected by Sunan, who came running. When the Brothers touched, I sent out a golden haze like the one you and Solange experienced. Afterwards, I could no longer detect an imbalance, but fatigue pulled me back into my body,*" related Tamara.

"*So you don't know how it affected them*?" asked Savea.

"*Sadly, no,*" sighed Tamara. "*After I've had a chance to rest and replenish my energy with food, I plan to find out.*"

Chapter 10
Sunan and Sostor, 2.0

When Tamara felt renewed and refreshed, she returned to her bed and prepared to revisit her grandfather. As she relaxed and let drowsiness overtake her, she felt herself being teleported once again to Mesarra.

Standing outside Sostor's cell, she noted with surprise that the door was open and the cell was empty. Wondering where the Brothers had gone, she decided to explore the dungeon. Moving from hallway to hallway, she found no trace of them. When she came to a stairway leading upwards, she climbed to the next level to continue her exploration.

Again finding only empty halls, she persisted and eventually came upon a room filled with comfortable furniture. Looking across that room, she spotted the Brothers sitting together and chatting in a friendly manner. Moving toward them, she sat in a chair close enough to hear their conversation.

Sostor was speaking, "Do you understand what has happened to us?"

"I do not," replied Sunan. "I remember finding out that there was a surge of magic in your cell. When I investigated and put the magic detection cuff on your arm, there was a great golden haze and we levitated into the air. Do you remember it that way?"

"Yes," agreed Sostor. "But before all that, why was I in a prison cell?"

"I don't know," answered Sunan. "Did you commit a crime?"

"I don't think so, but my memory is very hazy. And why were you checking my magic level—had it changed?"

"I'm very confused," Sunan claimed. "Why are you in my kingdom anyway? I don't remember inviting you."

"And I don't remember coming here," Sostor retorted.

* * * * *

Tamara decided that she had learned enough. The Brothers were clearly disoriented. She allowed herself to return to her bed and awaken. She found Savea once again sitting by her in a chair.

"*What did you find*?" asked Savea.

"*Sostor is no longer in a cell. The Brothers are sitting in a well-appointed room and comparing notes. They are both suffering memory loss and are confused about recent developments. I would question whether either of them recall what they have done, including my family's kidnapping and Soster's imprisonment*," proposed Tamara.

Solange entered the room and added, "*I heard what you just reported, Tamara. I recommend that we somehow figure out how to get the Brothers back here so we can all sit down together and work this out. Any ideas?*"

"*What if we have a reunion party? My family is back here safely and we could ask the Brothers to join us in celebrating. They may not remember the kidnapping, but we might learn something from that as well. I think the Commander might be able to help us with some magical interrogation,*" Tamara suggested. "*I'll send for him to join us at the boat.*"

"*And Trident's improving magical skills would be a wild card,*" said Savea. "*Neither Brother is aware of this new development. I think we should invite him as well.*"

* * * * *

At the boat, Tamara and the Sisters eagerly awaited the arrival of Trident and the Commander. When everyone was aboard, Tamara reiterated her astral journey findings so that everyone had the latest intel. Then she asked if there were any questions, reminding them to use mental communication.

"*It will be nice when we can actually speak again, but we still don't know who planted the listening devices. Although I suspect Sunan, I have no real evidence,*" she stressed.

"*I have a question,*" said Trident. "*Are you telling me*

that Sostor does not remember kidnapping us?"

"*I am,*" replied Tamara. "*We need to do something while they are here to restore their memories. Commander, can you help with that*?"

"*I believe so,*" the Commander replied. "*As I understand it, when the Sisters were restored from their imbalance, it took two attempts: one for each of the two spells that were cast.*"

"*You are correct,*" affirmed Tamara. "*So I need to repeat the spell I cast on the astral plane*?"

"*Exactly. And I will be there to assist you,*" said the Commander.

"*I'll issue the invitation to the Brothers immediately,*" promised Tamara. "*But what if one or both refuse?*"

"*Is there anything you can offer that would prevent that*?" asked the Commander.

Savea chuckled, "*Give me the invitations and I'll deliver them personally—clad in a very special spell I happen to know which compels obedience!*"

"*Brilliant!*" everyone applauded.

Chapter 11
The Reunion Celebration

Tamara stood at the doorway to the Private Dining Room, ready to welcome her guests. First to arrive, her family entered the room. She embraced her parents and sister, leading them to the attractively set table. "You're our guests of honor," she declared. "Please make yourselves comfortable."

Returning to the doorway, she spied the Commander approaching. "Where do you prefer to sit?" she asked.

"Facing the door," he stressed. "I need to be able to observe the room."

The next guests made a surprising entrance. The Sisters appeared, each on the arm of a Super Brother. Hiding her feelings, she welcomed them warmly and led them to the table. Since both suspects were now present, she switched to vocal communication, assuming that her previous sharing of mental communication with Sostor would probably allow him to overhear her private mental communication with her family. Gesturing to the chairs on either side of hers, she invited the Brothers to sit. The Sisters took chairs next to the Brothers.

After a delicious repast featuring sea bass and shrimp, they enjoyed a fruity dessert and after-dinner drinks.

Conversation around the table had been lively and pleasant. Tamara stood and offered a toast in celebration of her family's return.

"Return?" asked Sostor, rising to his feet and moving to stand next to Tamara. "Have they been on holiday?"

"I'm afraid it was nothing so pleasant," replied Tamara. "They were kidnapped on their way to the mainland."

"Kidnapped?!" exclaimed Sunan, also rising to stand next to his brother. "By whom?"

"That is yet to be determined," said the Commander as he walked around the table and stood behind the Brothers. Placing his hands on their shoulders, he started a soft chant. The Brothers turned to face him, confusion on their faces. Tamara stood and clasped their hands, adding her voice to the Commander's chant as he backed away.

The Brothers faced Tamara as her bracelets generated a golden haze around the three of them. Rising into the air, the three of them began to rotate. Soon Tamara was turning with a single Super Being. When the golden haze began to dissipate, they returned to the floor and the single Being once again became two. The Commander assisted the Brothers back to their chairs as the other dinner guests watched in amazement.

"I believe the imbalance has been corrected," Tamara pronounced. "How are you feeling?" she asked the Brothers.

"What did you do to us?" demanded Sostor.

"It wasn't harmful, Brother," contributed Sunan. "In fact, I had been feeling confused and my memory was foggy. Now I have clear memories. What about you?"

"I have to say I'm feeling much better," affirmed Sostor. "But I'm also experiencing sadness and shame. I fear that I was responsible for the kidnapping—and I don't understand why."

"You're not the only kidnapper at this table," admitted Sunan. "I have memories of kidnapping you—and I don't know why, either."

"Not that long ago," interjected Solange, "Savea and I were unable to get along. We had both fallen in love with the same man, and our relationship suffered. Tamara determined that we were suffering from an imbalance, which she helped to resolve. She just did the same for you."

"I suspect the emotional struggle between the two of you was also rooted in sibling rivalry," suggested Savea. "But instead of jealousy, yours was about ambition."

"What could have caused these imbalances?" asked Sostor.

"I think we might need to go all the way back to when we were one Super Being and then divided," proposed Sunan.

"I think you are on to something," agreed the Commander. "But before tackling such a huge challenge, I would recommend that you examine some of your past behaviors. For example, the possibly artificial former king and the wedding night Solange experienced. Then there were the attacks on Marinea both under the sea and from the air. I would be happy to assist you in recovering those memories if they prove to be elusive."

Sunan and Sostor looked at each other in confusion. "Those memories still seem to be blocked," Sunan admitted. "Brother, can you retrieve any?"

"Not yet," Sostor agreed. "Commander, how can you help us?"

"I have a degree in magical studies, and some of the spells I learned could be helpful. We need to free up your memories to determine what was true and real and what was artificially created," explained the Commander.

"I offer you the hospitality of Marinea," promised Tamara. "You can remain here while we attempt to understand what has happened to you and how to correct it."

The Brothers nodded gratefully and accepted her offer.

Chapter 12
Untangling the Web

The next morning, the four Super Children, Tamara, the Commander and Trident gathered at the boat for a strategy meeting. Tamara explained why the boat was necessary, since the perpetrator of the listening devices was still unknown. Then she asked if anyone had a question before they began the meeting. She did not urge mental communication since she was unsure whether the Brothers could eavesdrop.

Sostor cleared his throat and spoke first, "So much has happened between and among us that I'm wondering how much we can trust each other. Do we have any way to ensure trust?"

"I understand your apprehension. I can only ensure one thing," promised Tamara. "In my experience, when I have a need, my crystals manage to satisfy that need. I trust them completely."

"I'd like to start with the kings who were regarded as Trident's grandfather and father," Tamara proposed. "Collect your thoughts and memories for just a moment and then we can share what we remember."

"I have never met or seen any prior kings," stated the

Commander, "My first question is: Raise your hand if you believe that they were real persons." No one raised their hand.

"It seems to be unanimous that you believe they were some type of artificial beings," continued the Commander. "Why do you think so, and what type of avatars do you think they were?"

"Sunan, I remember that you told me their appearance was not distinct when you were at the coronation of Trident's father many years ago," prompted Tamara.

"Yes," said Sunan. "That was the only time I saw them, and it was from a distance. After the 'grandfather' king left the stage, I never saw him again. I wasn't sure if I had been drinking too much, so I ignored the impression."

"I saw my so-called father a couple of times when I was a child, but only from far away," contributed Trident. "I knew he was my father, but he never even talked to me. So when the king became ill and eventually died, it was my duty to assume the throne."

Sostor spoke next, "Like Sunan, I only encountered Trident's father once. I was in the back of a crowd at a formal ceremony. I was standing next to a beautiful woman, so my attention was not on the king. I'm sorry to not be of more help."

"I guess that leaves Solange and me," said Savea. "We were never invited to any ceremonies. While Solange and I were very instrumental in helping manage the kingdom for the king who was Trident's grandfather, he was never involved and we were regarded as staff."

Solange added, "I support what Savea shared. The only time I encountered the former king was on my wedding night and his appearance was hazy in my memory. After that, I was blindfolded."

The Commander sighed and said, "That really doesn't leave us much to go on, I'm afraid. Does anyone have more to add?"

"Yes," pressed Tamara. "Now that the Brothers have been released from their spells, they must have accurate memories to share. Let's return to Grandmother's wedding night. What were your roles that evening?"

"Before you answer," interrupted the Commander, "I want you to drink the potion in these two vials. It is designed to enhance truth and memory. Should either of you resist the potion in any way, it will turn your skin blue."

The Brothers looked at each other and shrugged. Reaching for the vials, they drank deeply and returned them empty to the Commander. There was no change in their skin color.

"I just remembered," confessed Sostor. "We were both at the wedding and also at the door to Solange's room in the evening. The former king, who we now believe was Trident's grandfather, attended the wedding in a large cloak with a hood. It was impossible to see his face. He was also present at Solange's door with his son, the bridegroom. Both of them were turned away from us so we could not view their faces.

"The next thing I knew, I was handed a glass of champagne and pushed into the room. Until now, I had remembered entering voluntarily and eagerly since I had a crush on Solange. But clearly, I was being manipulated without my true consent. It's also possible that the champagne was drugged. Sunan, what do you remember?"

"I was also given a glass, and I watched the king and his son walk swiftly down the hall, but after that I have no memory of the rest of the evening," responded Sunan.

"I seem to recall that you, my Brother, were in charge of shoving me through that door and encouraging me to make love to Solange. But now I realize that it is a false memory—probably induced by that glass of what I now believe was fake champagne," sighed Sostor. "However, I must admit that once I was with Solange, my own feelings and desires took over and I thoroughly enjoyed the experience!"

Sostor walked over to Trident and embraced him. "I suspected you were my son when you were kidnapped and arrived at my castle. You looked so much like me."

Trident stepped back and looked searchingly at Sostor. "About that kidnapping…"

Chapter 13
The Kidnapping, 2.0

Sostor led Trident to a chair and asked him to sit down. Joining him, he pleaded, "Son, I understand your anger and it's completely justified. But I am begging you to have patience and help us understand what has happened and why. I'm beginning to believe that there is something much larger at play here."

Sunan echoed his brother's plea. "And I want to add that while I was visiting Marinea, I worked with Tamara to remove the two spells that had created the imbalance in the Super Sisters. At that time, we had no idea that Sostor and I were similarly affected by two imbalance spells."

Tamara summed up: "We don't know who or why those spells were cast on the Super Children, but we intend to find out. Meanwhile, this is what we know.

"Both sets of spells were cast to produce strong impulses of competition. For the Sisters, the competition focused on jealousy, specifically on fighting over the same man. For the Brothers, the competition was for power—in this case, the drive to take control of your kingdom in order to outperform the other Brother."

"With that background in mind, we must examine the behavior of Sunan and Sostor during the time when the spells were active," pressed Savea.

"Yes," agreed Sostor. "It is true that I arranged the kidnapping of Trident and his family in the hope that I could convince him to abdicate in my favor. At that time, I did not know he was my son, although I suspected. With what I now know, I am so proud of his refusal to submit to my clumsy efforts to force him to my will."

"Do you remembering threatening him and adding torture to the persuasion attempt?" asked Tamara.

Sostor thought for a minute and then said uncertainly, "Actually, I don't. Why is that?"

The Commander interrupted, "I think I can answer your question. What Tamara observed in her astral journeys appears to have been an artificial replica of you doing that intimidation. But I don't know where you were during that time."

"I can help there. When I found that Sostor was no longer a willing participant in our plot, I kidnapped him and substituted the avatar." contributed Sunan, "I created robot armies to abduct Sostor and attack Marinea via the clever tunnel that the Sisters erected. Plus, let's not forget that aerial attack I launched against your kingdom, Tamara. My apologies for all of it. However, I don't believe that Sostor and I had any part in the wedding night debacle—except for Soster's enthusiastic participation, that is!"

"So, Son," asked Sostor, "Can you find it in your heart to forgive an unknowing and temporarily manipulative father for what now looks like a series of unforgivable actions?"

"Given what we have learned, Sostor," answered Trident, "I definitely forgive you. Can you explain why you were so jealous of Sunan?"

"Sure," he answered, "First of all, he ruled a warm kingdom populated by happy people. And I was given a frozen kingdom with citizens who were faced with so many challenges just to survive. I did my best to create a structure that would be successful, but there was a lot of local resentment. So, even without the spells, there was a lot of rivalry between us."

"That leaves us with intriguing questions," said the Commander. "Who orchestrated this complex plot involving all four Super Children? And why? Certainly the relationships between the two Sisters and the two Brothers produced fertile ground for those spells to take root."

"Well, now that we understand the Brothers' behaviors as the Commander has summarized, we need to examine the larger picture," proposed Tamara. "Since my crystals have not activated in any way, I must assume that everything that has been revealed today is the truth. I would like the Super Children to reflect and gather any information that may aid our future deliberations. I recommend that we reconvene here tomorrow after breakfast to consider what may be fueling what we have discussed today."

* * * * *

The next day, after enjoying a good night's rest and a breakfast of pancakes and shrimp, the group proceeded to the boat to continue their analysis of recent events.

"It has become apparent," began Tamara, "that none of us were involved in initiating this complex plot. That raises the questions: who was? And why?"

Solange proposed a possible scenario, "We all know our cosmology. As I remember it, the Super Beings decided to make offspring. Why?" Were they bored? They didn't seem to be doing so out of affection for each other. Then they created the four of us by dividing their two original children to prevent them from holding too much power. What were they afraid of?"

"And after they threw that asteroid at us because they didn't like non-magical people viewing us as deities, we four Super Children combined our powers to deflect it. Were they jealous?" asked Savea. "Then the Great Quakes occurred and the single land mass was divided up. What was their motivation for that?"

"Finally, they allocated pieces of land above and below the sea to us with the mission of caring for the planet as 'part of our education'. Why was that necessary?" asked Sunan.

"Do we all agree on this proposed scenario so far?" inquired the Commander.

The four Super Children nodded. "But then what?" asked Sostor. "Where are you going with this scenario, Solange?"

Solange continued, "What if the Super Beings again became bored? What if they decided to create a game to amuse themselves? What if we became pawns in that game? What if this complex plot we've been living through is part of that game's design?"

Sunan groaned and said, "So many 'what if's'"

Tamara interjected, "My crystals are still quiet, telling me that what you are suggesting may be true. Did those Super Being Parents ever show you any love or affection? The only emotions I've been able to identify are boredom, jealousy, and anger. For now, let's try assuming that Solange has it right. Let's reconvene at breakfast tomorrow—after individually considering the various angles of her scenario and what might be our next logical moves."

Tamara stood and exited the boat. The Super Children

sat quietly for a short time and followed her off.

Trident and the Commander remained on the boat, looking at each other thoughtfully. The Commander sighed and said, "Let the games begin."

About the Author

After doing academic writing during my 20 years as Professor at the University of Wisconsin-Madison, I retired to Hawai'i in 1999. A decade later, I began being aware of an interesting fantasy story line in my mind and began writing it soon after. It was an occasional hobby for another decade and then the book became impatient with me and began to seriously nudge me. Since I began "listening" to the book, the writing has been a fun and all-encompassing part of my life.

Crystal Saga Series
by
D. E. Weingand

Book 1

Tamara's Crystals

Book 2

Genesis Explored

Book 3

Masquerade

Book 4

Discoveries

Scan the QR Code with Your Cell Phone to Order Books

Coming Soon

Book 5
Gamesmanship

Book 6
Beginnings

Book 7
Looking Forward . . . and Backward

Book 8
Making Progress

www.ingramcontent.com/pod-product-compliance
Lightning Source LLC
LaVergne TN
LVHW050645100826
845148LV00011B/1982

9780578349664